48043

Upton, Robert.

Fade out

✓
4/96
6/98

Also by Robert Upton

Who'd Want to Kill Old George?
(An Amos McGuffin mystery)

A Golden Fleecing

FADE OUT

AN AMOS McGUFFIN MYSTERY

ROBERT UPTON

THE VIKING PRESS   NEW YORK

Copyright © 1984 by Robert Upton
All rights reserved
First published in 1984 by The Viking Press
40 West 23rd Street, New York, N.Y. 10010
Published simultaneously in Canada by
Penguin Books Canada Limited

LIBRARY OF CONGRESS CATALOGING IN PUBLICATION DATA
Upton, Robert.
Fade out.
I. Title.
PS3571.P5F3   1984   813′.54   83-40225
ISBN 0-670-30469-7

Printed in the United States of America
Set in Caledonia

For Kathleen and Jeffrey

1

It was the week of the film festival and the streets of San Francisco were filled with cinéastes. Even Goody's bar, usually a forum for local politicians, lawyers, judges, cops, and certain members of the Fourth Estate, found itself host to a few of them. They were huddled around one of the cigarette-burned card tables opposite the long mahogany bar when McGuffin walked in. They were tossing foreign names across the table like cards—"I'll see your Rohmer and raise you one Kurosawa."

"What the hell are they talkin' about?" Goody asked, planting the bottle of Paddy's in front of McGuffin. "Foreign cars?"

"They're cinéastes," McGuffin explained, as Goody, unbidden, poured the whiskey. It was understood that McGuffin didn't drink while on a case, but he hadn't had a client in weeks and his eyes showed it.

"A cinéaste," Goody repeated, eyeing the table suspiciously. "What's that—somebody who likes little boys?" He should have known—anybody who'd order Perrier.

McGuffin shook his head. "That's a pederast."

"I thought that was somebody who liked feet."

"That's a podiatrist," McGuffin explained. Holding his glass with three fingers, he raised it slowly and delicately, then knocked it back with a quick flip.

"The way McGuffin drinks whiskey, it's a thing of beauty," Goody had often observed; "until his fifteenth or twentieth, then he gets a little sloppy."

But now McGuffin was only on his first, having spent the early hours of the evening at a French festival entry, whose title he had already forgotten. He had enjoyed it—he liked most French movies as much as he disliked most American movies—except for Bogart. There was the exception.

It was probably because of Bogart and the piles of detective pulp he had devoured as a youth that McGuffin had become a private eye. He would always remember the words of some now forgotten detective that, at the tender age of eleven, had forever sealed his professional destiny:

> It was late and I was fagged, so I decided to stack a few Z's on the old office chesterfield. The last sheep had just cleared the fence when she busted in—and I mean busted!—a platinum blonde, built like a Maginot bunker, and naked under a long chinchilla coat.

Naked under a chinchilla coat...It was the sort of image that, once implanted in an impressionable young mind, would remain there forever, influencing decisions both big and small. Those of little imagination might choose to build shopping malls or juggle numbers on columned sheets, but not young Amos McGuffin. For he had, at an all too early age, been exposed to steamy women and smoking guns and was irretrievably lost to the dull world of commerce. He would be a private eye.

Of course the practice proved considerably different from the youthful fantasy, and McGuffin often wished he had become a movie-actor detective with a baggy suit and forties felt hat and a cigarette hanging from a moist lower lip instead of the knocked-about, shot-at, real thing. But all in all, he had few regrets over the line of work he had chosen. True, the money wasn't much, but there were occasional satisfactions that he had so far observed in few other occupations—certainly not among the lawyers and judges who bellied up to Goody's bar each evening after wrestling with such lofty legal issues as Who entered the intersection first? Unlike these jaded professionals, McGuffin still perceived his duty with something of the innocent clarity of romantic youth—get the bad guy.

At that he was unrelenting. Sometimes clumsy, but always unrelenting. McGuffin derived a certain amount of pleasure from helping a client in distress, but he knew—and he worried that it might be a weakness of character—that his greatest satisfaction by far came from nailing the bad guy. Had he been born a hundred years earlier, McGuffin might well have been a vigilante, not a detective.

McGuffin started to drink, then replaced his glass, suddenly aware that Goody was watching him closely from across the bar.

"What's the matter?" McGuffin asked.

"You look terrible," Goody replied.

McGuffin studied his face in the yellowing mirror behind the bar, rubbing his fingers lightly over the red stubble on his pale cheeks. Maybe the face was a little puffy, but the cheekbones still showed through, and his brick-colored hair was still reasonably thick. All in all, it wasn't a bad face for man pushing forty, McGuffin decided, unable to remember if he was thirty-six or thirty-seven. It was a sort of Huckleberry Finn face that would, if McGuffin didn't push it too hard, maintain its youthful quality for a good many years. A few days in the sun and a good workout, McGuffin thought, giving his paunch an affectionate pat, and I'll look like a movie star.

"I don't think I look so bad," McGuffin said, raising the glass to his mirror image.

He swallowed the whiskey with a satisfied sigh, then slid the glass across the bar to Goody, who snatched it up in a lumpy, broken-knuckled hand. Goody had been his own bouncer for more than thirty years and his hands and nose showed it. He resembled a beer keg with a torpedo head resting on top, but no one except McGuffin had ever dared point that out. Goody could be a tough sonofabitch or a soft touch. To McGuffin he was a veritable Jewish mother.

"I suppose you want another," the barkeep grumbled. It was a peculiar but familiar refrain—the bar owner disapproving of the customer's habit. But Goody's was an unusual bar.

"You buying?" McGuffin asked.

"I'll put it on your tab, that's probably the same thing," Goody answered, tossing the ice into the sink. He doused the glass in water, scooped more ice into it, and splashed in a bit of Paddy's. Goody poured as well, as McGuffin drank.

"Thanks," McGuffin said, when Goody clanked the glass on the bar in front of him.

"For nothin'," Goody muttered. He watched as McGuffin sipped his drink, then asked: "Any prospects?"

McGuffin shook his head. "If I don't get a client pretty soon, I'll become an alcoholic."

Goody said nothing. The fact that McGuffin drank only between cases meant less and less as his periods of unemployment lengthened.

The girl from the table of cinéastes approached the bar with three empty Perrier bottles and Goody waddled down the bar to help her as Tommy, the Chinese paperboy, staggered in, a stuffed newspaper sack over one shoulder and a shoeshine box over the over.

"Shine? *Examiner?*" he asked, as he made his way down the bar.

The girl bought a paper and tucked it under her arm while she waited for Goody to return with her three Perriers.

"What's with the shoe box?" McGuffin asked, handing the boy two quarters for the paper. "Isn't there enough money in the newspaper business?"

"You gotta diversify," Tommy said, folding and handing the paper to McGuffin. "You want a shine?"

"I can't afford it. If you need an assistant, give me a call," McGuffin said, as the boy started for the door.

McGuffin placed the newspaper on the bar, just as a sudden commotion broke out among the cinéastes at the table behind him. They were huddled over the newspaper, babbling excitedly at the headlines. McGuffin flopped his paper open to the front page and looked for himself.

PRODUCER DISAPPEARS!
SUICIDE OR HOAX?

Ben Volper, a Hollywood film producer, was thought to
have waded into the Pacific Ocean and drowned himself
on Sunday afternoon after leaving an unsigned suicide note
in his typewriter.

"Who the hell is Ben Volper?" McGuffin wondered aloud.

"Who is Ben Volper?" came the incredulous reply from
the cinéastes, as if they were a rusty barbershop quartet.

McGuffin swung around on the bar stool for instruction.

"Ben Volper is a genius," proclaimed a serious-looking
young man in a frayed field jacket stuffed with magazines
and notebooks. "He's the man who produced *Lemmings*."

"*Lemmings?*"

The young man shook his head sadly. "It was the opening
entry in this year's festival."

"Oh yeah," McGuffin remembered. "I read the reviews."

"The popular reviewers didn't understand it," the young
man's girl friend said.

"*Plague Stew* didn't do well at the box office, either, but
now it's considered to be one of the few masterpieces of
American cinema, at least by most *serious* critics," the one
with the beard added.

"I missed that one, too," McGuffin admitted.

"He's not for everybody," the girl friend added.

"Probably not," McGuffin said, and turned around to read
his paper.

He recognized a few of Volper's more commercial pictures, and remembered that he had rather liked them. His
first movie, *Fields of Flesh,* had starred the Swedish actress
Jenny Lang, "the most voluptuous woman in Hollywood,"
who later became his wife. They were, McGuffin was surprised to read, still married. No Bogart, she had nevertheless
been one of McGuffin's favorites while he was growing up.

"Remember Jenny Lang?" McGuffin asked Goody.

Goody stopped pumping the beer glass and cupped his
wet hands in front of him. "Big tits?"

"That's the one."

"I saw her on cable the other night, wading around in some Italian fountain. Humongous!"

"You're thinking of Anita Ekberg," McGuffin corrected.

Goody didn't hear. "A broad that big, she shoulda been declared a national recreation area. Why would anybody married to a woman like that wanna commit suicide?"

"Sex isn't everything," McGuffin said, as Goody started down the bar for the ringing phone.

And you should know, McGuffin spoke silently to his reflection in the mirror. For he had been married to a sex symbol, a long-legged, wasp-waisted blonde, who, at the time he first met her, in a place called the No-Name Bar, was living on a houseboat in Sausalito and painting bad abstract art. She was standing alone at the bar when McGuffin walked in, saw her, and decided almost at that instant that he would marry her. It was an insane decision, purely chemical, but when their eyes met, McGuffin knew instinctively that she had decided the same thing and so it must be all right. A moment later her date returned to the bar, but McGuffin was no more dismayed by this than by the fact that he too had a date, an attractive young schoolteacher with whom he had just spent a wonderful weekend at Squaw Valley.

McGuffin and the schoolteacher took a table next to the wall, where he absently sipped his drink and waited for his chance, patient as a moray eel. It came when she walked to the jukebox. McGuffin excused himself and followed her to the jukebox, not knowing what he would do or what he would say, but somehow supremely confident that he would be successful. When he stood beside her, their hips touched. Thinking back, he couldn't remember who was responsible, but the flush of excitement was still vivid.

"I'm going to take my date home and I'll be back here in half an hour," he had said. "Where will you be?"

"Right here," she had answered, still studying the selections.

"What about your friend at the bar?" he asked.

"What friend?" she answered.

When McGuffin returned, she was alone. A short while later they were married and McGuffin, who hated boats, moved aboard hers. Several years later, after their daughter was born and after the divorce, McGuffin learned that sex isn't everything.

Funny, McGuffin thought, that a guy who hates boats should be living on one again. Although it was no Sausalito houseboat this time, to be sure, but a large ferryboat, the old *Oakland Queen*, tied at the Embarcadero, not far from Ghirardelli Square, and converted to a posh floating office building. McGuffin had a combination home and office in the wheelhouse, rent-free, in exchange for acting as the night security guard. It was a demeaning job for a private eye of McGuffin's caliber, but it would only be temporary, just until he made his killing. So far he had been there almost five years.

"Amos, telephone!" Goody called from the end of the bar.

"Who is it?" McGuffin asked, walking to the pay phone. It couldn't be a job—his business number was the boat.

"Your answering service."

"Answering service! I don't have an answering service."

"Search me." Goody shrugged and handed him the phone. "But it sounds like that old Mrs. Begelman."

"Yes, it's that old Mrs. Begelman!" came a shrill but familiar voice as McGuffin lifted the receiver to his ear. "And you can tell him I heard."

"Jesus—" McGuffin whispered. He hadn't had an answering service in more than a year, not since Mrs. Begelman had cut him off for nonpayment. "If it's about the money—" McGuffin began.

"It's not about the money," she interrupted. "At least not yet. All evening I've been calling your number and what am I getting? An answering machine. You can't pay me a lousy fifteen dollars a month, but an answering machine yet, you can afford. You're some big shot, aren't you? So just tell me, when you got an answering service, what do you need with an answering machine? Are you trying to add insult to injury yet?"

"Wait, wait a minute, Mrs. Begelman," McGuffin cut in testily. "It just so happens that I was forced to go to Macy's and charge that answering machine because you—you, Mrs. Begelman, you stony-hearted yenta—you cut off my service."

"Do you mind, Mr. McGuffin, can we talk like civilized people? Of course I cut off your service. Because you don't pay me for seven months I cut off your service. You call that unreasonable?"

"It wasn't *that* long," McGuffin protested.

"It wasn't that long—you want to know the exact date? I got it right here."

"No, I don't want to know the exact date. Look, Mrs. Begelman, if it's not about the money and I'm not on service anymore, why are you calling me?"

"I'm calling because I got a long-distance call for you that looks like it might be a very big job."

"A job?" McGuffin gasped. "Who? Who called, Mrs. Begelman?"

"Uh-uh, Mr. McGuffin. You've got your fancy-shmancy new answering machine. Why should you ask an old yenta who called?"

"Mrs. Begelman, please," McGuffin pleaded. "I'm sorry if I offended you. I haven't paid for the answering machine; I'll bring it back first thing tomorrow. I'll go back on service, just like old times."

"And you'll pay me everything you owe me?"

"Every last cent, I promise. Just as soon as I get paid, you get paid."

"Don't forget your tab!" Goody hollered.

McGuffin waved him quiet, then spoke urgently into the mouthpiece. "Tell me, Mrs. Begelman, who called?"

She let him hang for a few moments before replying. "His name is Volpersky," she finally answered. "V-O-L-P-E-R-S-K-Y."

McGuffin threw his notebook open on the bar and scratched in the name, followed by the New York phone number she recited. "Thank you, Mrs. Begelman. Thank you from the bottom of my heart."

"So when do I get paid?" she asked.

"Before the end of the month," he promised.

"Before the end of the week," she countered.

"Next week," he bargained.

"Done," she agreed, and rang off.

McGuffin hung up and quickly frisked himself for change. Finding none, he called: "Goody, give me a handful of quarters and put it on my tab, will you?"

"Why don't you use your credit card?" Goody grumbled as he punched the cash register.

"Ma Bell has temporarily suspended my privileges," McGuffin explained, reaching for the money as Goody approached. It was his first prospect in weeks and he was becoming noticeably excited.

Muttering, Goody splashed a handful of quarters on the bar. One of the coins rolled slowly across the mahogany, like a skater on ice, pirouetted, and collapsed. McGuffin dropped a coin into the phone and dialed the number, then, at the operator's instruction, jammed several more quarters into the box. The phone was picked up on the first ring.

"Yes, this is Volpersky," McGuffin was assured, after he had identified himself. The voice was quick and choppy, with a slight middle-European accent. It also bore the familiar nervous ring of a prospective client in distress. McGuffin's pulse quickened. "You don't know me, but Schwartz the deli man, my only friend in California, he told me to call you."

"Izzy Schwartz?" McGuffin asked. He owned a delicatessen on Geary in the theater district. One night McGuffin threw a couple of punks out of his place by pretending to be a cop, and Izzy, by way of gratitude, stood McGuffin to a corned beef sandwich once in a while.

"Yeah, Izzy," Mr. Volpersky answered. "We were kids together in the Bronx. Izzy says you're a good detective."

"Very good," McGuffin said.

"He also says you're *totally* meshugge and you drink too much."

"I'm not totally meshugge," McGuffin said defensively.

"What about the drinking?"

"And I never drink when I'm on a case."

"Okay," Mr. Volpersky said, apparently satisfied. "You know my son, he's a big macher in the movie business. Only he calls himself Volper—like he couldn't spell sky."

McGuffin glanced at the newspaper on the bar. "The producer who—!"

"Committed suicide?" he said, mercifully completing McGuffin's thought. "Don't you believe it, Mr. McGuffin. Ben is a good boy, solid as a rock. Banks give him millions of dollars. I ask you, is that the kind of boy who would commit suicide?"

"I wouldn't think so," McGuffin mumbled absently, thinking exactly the opposite. It's hard to feel suicidal when banks are giving you millions of dollars, but it could be severely depressing should they stop.

"I saw Ben only a few weeks ago. He comes to see me whenever he's in New York. Believe me, a better son I couldn't ask—never gave me any trouble. If anything is bothering him, he tells me, always has. And believe me, Mr. McGuffin, nothing is bothering my Ben. He's happily married to a beautiful woman—a shiksa but very nice. I've never seen him happier."

"I see," McGuffin said, stacking quarters on the bar. "Then why would he want to disappear?"

"I'm trying to tell you—he *wouldn't* want to disappear," Volpersky replied.

McGuffin tended to agree. Ben Volper's disappearance was beginning to look more and more like a publicity stunt, as well as a terribly cruel joke on a loving father. But that was Hollywood, where hype mattered far more than filial obligation.

"What would you like me to do?" McGuffin asked, carefully placing the last quarter on the top of the stack. The pile was two knuckles high.

"Do? I want you to find him!" Mr. Volpersky exclaimed. "Why else am I calling a detective?"

"Right," McGuffin agreed. "Did Izzy mention my fee?"

"I can pay, don't worry about that," Volpersky assured him, neither boast nor bullshit. McGuffin liked the sound of it, there was money in the tone. "How much do you get?"

"Three hundred dollars a day plus expenses," McGuffin answered, trying to sound casual but firm.

"Three hundred!" the old man shouted. "Izzy tells me you work for chopped liver. Three hundred a day I don't call chopped liver."

Goody, watching from a few feet off, gestured anxiously but silently for McGuffin to reduce his price. Negotiations, McGuffin realized, were at a delicate stage. But he sensed money. For the record, his fee was fixed, while in actuality it fluctuated wildly between penury and wishful thinking.

"There are cheaper detectives," McGuffin informed him, his standard reply. "But I work quickly, bill honestly, and get results."

Mr. Volpersky wasn't impressed. "I'll go two hundred, no more," he insisted.

"I never cut fees," McGuffin replied in a dignified tone. "But because this case intrigues me, I'll take two-fifty with a twenty-five hundred advance."

Again Volpersky was not impressed. "Fifteen hundred, because I'm intrigued too," he countered.

McGuffin was about to ask for two thousand when the operator cut in and asked for two dollars more. McGuffin knocked his column of coins over, then hastily gathered them up and stuffed eight of them into the phone.

"You're calling from a pay phone?" Volpersky exclaimed incredulously.

"I'm in the field—on a case," McGuffin answered hastily. "I'll settle for the fifteen hundred. Where do I send the contract?"

"Only if you like. I don't need a contract," Volpersky said. "Izzy tells me you're too dumb to steal."

"I must thank Izzy," McGuffin muttered, turning to a clean page in his notebook. He printed Ben Volper's name in block letters across the top of the page. "Now I'd like some information about your son and anybody who might know where he is."

"I've got all that right here," Volpersky said. "Jenny Lang, his wife, you must know."

"Of course," McGuffin said, writing her name and address near the top of the page. Every red-blooded American boy over thirty knew Jenny Lang.

"And Judy Sloan?"

"Who is Judy Sloan?"

"Judith Slutzsky."

"Pardon me?"

"Judy Sloan is really Judith Slutzsky," Mr. Volpersky explained. "In Hollywood everything is made up, especially the names. Judith's father I'm knowing for more than fifty years. He runs the kosher butcher shop around the corner. But his daughter has to change her name because she's representing all the big stars. You think she can bring her father out to meet Barbra Streisand once in a while? Not a chance. Listen to me, Mr. McGuffin, you get to be a big detective, God forbid you should forget your parents."

"I won't," McGuffin promised. "Who else you got on your list?"

"Mark Drumm, with two m's."

He needn't have mentioned it. Mark Drumm had once been a big star, but McGuffin hadn't heard or seen much of him in the past several years. "Mark Drumm," he repeated, as he added the name to the list.

"Drumm shrumm," the old man muttered. "He's farshtinkener Marvin Dumbrowski from the building next door. My Ben was friends with his older brother."

"Wait a minute," McGuffin said, dropping his pen on the bar. "Are all Ben's friends from the old neighborhood?"

"Who else can you trust?" Volpersky answered. "Hollywood is a shark tank, big fish eating little fish. These kids, they get together at Ben's house every Sunday, nobody trying to make a nickel off anybody else. It's the only thing that keeps Ben sane in that meshuggeneh town."

"You sound like you know them pretty well," McGuffin observed.

"I see them whenever I'm out there, once or twice a year. I told you, Ben's a good boy and he's got nice friends."

"Who are the others?"

"Isaac Stein, the director, and David Hochman, the writer.

They're the only ones, God bless them, didn't change their names when they left the old neighborhood."

"What about Jenny Lang? You aren't going to tell me she's from the old neighborhood, are you?" McGuffin asked.

"No. Jenny was already a star when Ben got there. But everybody else, Ben made them stars—Drumm, Stein, Hochman, Judy—Ben made them all stars. They adore the guy."

"What about enemies, does he have any?"

"None that I ever heard of. Ben's one of those people you can't help liking, was always that way. And the girls— he used to have to beat them off with a stick."

"Okay, Mr. Volpersky," McGuffin said, closing his notebook. "I'll fly down to Los Angeles and have a look around."

"You think you can find him?" Volpersky asked. It was the first note of uncertainty McGuffin had detected in the old man.

"Yeah, I'll find him," McGuffin promised. He just hoped he could find Volper before he decided to turn himself in, so he wouldn't feel guilty about taking the old man's money. "You can wire me the advance care of the *Oakland Queen,* the Embarcadero."

"*Oakland Queen?* What the hell is that?" Volpersky asked.

"It's a ferryboat. I have my office and apartment there," McGuffin explained.

"He lives on a ferryboat," the old man remarked to no one. "Izzy told me you were meshugge."

"I'll call you just as soon as I've got something," McGuffin promised.

"Thank you, Mr. McGuffin," Volpersky said. The voice sounded suddenly soft and far away.

"You're welcome," McGuffin said. He said good-bye and slowly replaced the receiver, then turned to Goody. "What's my tab?"

Goody shrugged. "Five hundred?"

"You'll get it tomorrow," McGuffin said.

"Congratulations!" Goody exclaimed, sweeping the bottle of Paddy's from the bar.

"Uh-uh," McGuffin said, covering his glass. "I'm on a case."

It had been a long time.

2

Early the next afternoon, with most of Mr. Volpersky's money riding on his hip (less his five-hundred-dollar bar bill), McGuffin boarded the commuter in San Francisco and flew to Los Angeles, where he rented a car at the airport and drove to the Beverly Hills Hotel, hostelry to the stars. Were he in search of a less glamorous missing person, McGuffin might have stayed at a cheap hotel on Wilshire Boulevard; but for a movie mogul, nothing less than the Beverly Hills would do, he rationalized. Besides, he had always wanted to see the Polo Lounge.

"I'm afraid I see nothing for a Mr. McGuffin," the man at the desk said, running his neatly manicured nails down a long list of reservations.

"But my secretary made a reservation," McGuffin said.

"I could put you in one of the bungalows, but it *is* more expensive," he warned.

"I'll take it," McGuffin replied unhesitatingly. Who did this fellow think he was dealing with? Ordinarily McGuffin was cautious regarding expenses. But in this case, once Ben Volper produced himself, McGuffin intended to make sure Volper reimbursed his father for all the expenses this stunt had cost him. It was the least the thoughtless sonofabitch could do, worrying his old man as he had.

The registration completed, the desk clerk signaled to a hovering bellhop, who snatched McGuffin's bag from the floor and led him out of the lobby and along a winding path that smelled of orange blossoms and eucalyptus. McGuffin's

14

bungalow was among the first cluster of pink buildings grouped in and along the edge of a stand of tall trees. The bungalows faced a broad expanse of lawn and, beyond that, a street of opulent houses that sloped gently down to Sunset Boulevard. He could park his car on the street and walk directly to the bungalow if for any reason he wanted to avoid the front desk, McGuffin realized.

"These places must be very popular with married men," he observed, as the bellhop unlocked the door.

"You got it," the young man replied with a quick nod as he opened the door.

There were two double beds in a carpeted room with draperies to the floor and a handsome writing table with hotel stationery neatly stacked in a tray, not at all the sort of thing McGuffin was used to. He waited patiently while the boy explained how the draperies worked then, feeling flush, tipped him five dollars. The moment the boy left, McGuffin removed his jacket and lunged for the phone.

"Desk," a female voice answered.

"The Judy Sloan Agency," McGuffin requested. "I don't have the number."

"It won't do you any good, she's in the lounge."

"The lounge?"

"The Polo Lounge." She sighed. What kind of idiot was she dealing with?

"Then connect me to the Polo Lounge," McGuffin instructed.

McGuffin heard the page and, a moment later, a somehow familiar, mellifluous male voice came over the line.

"Judy's on another line, would you like to hold?" the velvet-voiced stranger inquired.

Suddenly McGuffin had it. "You didn't learn to talk like that in the Bronx," he said.

"Who is this?" Mark Drumm, the movie star, demanded.

"My name is Amos McGuffin. I'm looking for Ben Volper."

There was a short pause. "Are you a cop?"

"Private. Mr. Volpersky hired me to find his son. I'd like to talk to you and Miss Sloan."

"Just a minute," he said, and covered the mouthpiece. He was off the phone for more than a minute. "I'm sorry," he said when he came back on, "but that won't be possible right now."

"When?" McGuffin asked.

"We need this phone," the actor said, and the line went dead.

McGuffin looked at the offending phone and shrugged. Then he rose, slipped back into his San Francisco–weight tweed jacket, and left the bungalow.

He returned to the lobby and entered a large, empty dining room, plainly not the Polo Lounge. A man in a tuxedo stepped out from behind a screen as McGuffin backed out of the room. He descended some narrow, carpeted stairs, past a soda counter, and down a glass-walled corridor of elegant shops until he was once again outside. Damned if I'll ask where the Polo Lounge is, he vowed, as he plunged on down the tree-shaded path to—the swimming pool. The tiled shore was dotted with bright yellow umbrellas and nearly naked bodies, burnished to the luster of fine persimmon golf clubs. Everybody seemed to be talking on the phone to everybody else. A deeply tanned young man stared curiously from the ticket booth at the fish-belly-white man in the dark tweed suit.

"Can I help you, sir?" he asked politely.

He looked as if he could be trusted. "Can you tell me how to get to the Polo Lounge?" McGuffin asked.

"Back inside and upstairs, sir, just off the lobby."

This time McGuffin found it. It was disappointing, small and uncharacteristically dark for Los Angeles, with a tiny bar and vinyl banquettes.

"May I help you?" the maître d' asked, peering over the top of his reading glasses at McGuffin's suit. A New York writer, he decided.

"I'm meeting Mark and Judy," McGuffin said, waving casually to no one. "Never mind, I see them," he said, spying the familiar, finely chiseled head of Mark Drumm, contrasting sharply against the clouds of blond hair that would be Judy Sloan.

"Sir!" the maître d' called, and hurried after McGuffin.

Judy Sloan was still on the phone; Mark Drumm was sipping Heineken from a bottle, staring curiously through round dark glasses at the man approaching their table.

"Miss Sloan," McGuffin demanded, planting himself firmly in front of her table, which was strewn with slips of paper with large numbers scribbled on them and an ashtray filled with cigarette butts.

"Miss Sloan is on the phone," Mark Drumm drawled lazily.

"I'm sorry, Mr. Drumm," the maître d' apologized.

Judy Sloan removed the phone and regarded McGuffin as she might a flasher.

"What the hell do you want?" she demanded hoarsely, a long brown cigarette bouncing at the corner of her mouth.

"My name is Amos McGuffin, I called a few—"

"No, I'm not talking to you!" she shouted into the phone. "I'm being assaulted by a fucking character actor in the Polo Lounge. Just leave your picture and résumé, will you, dear?" she said, showing McGuffin a long, even row of capped teeth.

"I'm not an actor, I'm a private detective, investigating the disappearance of Ben Volper," he informed her.

"I told you," Mark Drumm said, beginning to rise. "We can't talk to you now."

"Don't get up," McGuffin said pleasantly, laying a heavy hand on the actor's shoulder. When he tried to rise, McGuffin squeezed his clavicle and forced him back into the banquette.

"Sonofabitch," Drumm muttered, rubbing his shoulder and glaring balefully at the detective.

"I'm afraid you'll have to leave," the maître d' implored.

"Not until I've had a few words with Miss Sloan and Mr. Drumm," McGuffin said, staring evenly into the actor's dark glasses. Now he might be an over-the-hill movie actor, but he was still a tough New York street kid who did not suffer such indignity lightly, McGuffin recognized.

"I'll call you back," Judy Sloan said, and slammed the

receiver in its cradle. "Get these phones out of here," she ordered, waving the maître d' away.

His arms piled with phones and dangling wires, the maître d' made his escape, as McGuffin slid into the banquette, squeezing the actor between himself and the agent.

"Thanks," McGuffin said, gazing around the room. There were a couple of vaguely familiar faces, but no stars. Most of the crowd was middle-aged, tanned, and trim, with sunglasses resting on top of their heads.

"I would have been happy to talk to you later," the agent said, the words rolling out resentfully on a hot cloud of smoke.

"This won't take long," McGuffin promised, patting his pockets for his notebook. He had left it, he remembered, in the bungalow beside the phone.

"It isn't time, it's timing," she informed him. "Right now Mark happens to be a very hot property."

"Because of Ben Volper's disappearance?"

"That has nothing to do with it," she snapped. "Can we get on with this?"

"I don't understand," McGuffin said, shaking his head. "Mr. Volpersky said you were all good friends, you got together every Sunday at Ben's house."

"So?" Mark Drumm said, talking around his beer bottle.

"So why aren't you being more cooperative? Don't you want to find him? Or do you happen to know that the whole thing is a publicity stunt?"

"It's not a publicity stunt," the agent replied firmly. "If it was, I'd know. I'm Ben's agent."

"Then do you think he could have committed suicide?"

"Anybody could have committed suicide, couldn't they?" she answered. "And when you find a man's clothes piled neatly on the beach and no sign of the man, that would seem to be a fair assumption, wouldn't it?"

"And a suicide note," Drumm added.

"Anybody could have typed that note," McGuffin said. "And if anybody other than Ben Volper did type it, then we're talking about murder."

Close-up—Horrified reactions. I would have made a great

director, McGuffin thought—if I weren't already such a crackerjack detective.

"Who'd want to kill old Ben?" Mark Drumm scoffed.

"Yeah, who?" McGuffin said. He couldn't get a reading on Drumm, hidden away as he was behind dark glasses. And Judy Sloan was too shrewd a flesh dealer to betray her feelings. "Does he have any enemies?"

"No more than any other powerful Hollywood producer," Judy Sloan said, grinding her cigarette out.

"Who are they?"

"Financial people mostly," she said, tapping another long brown cigarette out of a red pack. Mark Drumm lit it for her and she exhaled sibilantly. "It's no secret, Ben's last few pictures haven't done too well at the box office. None of the majors would back *Lemmings*, all I could get was a negative pickup."

"What's that?" McGuffin asked. It sounded like the last girl in a singles bar at closing time.

"That means they'll only bid on the film after it's finished. It was up to Ben to raise the money from outside sources."

"And where did he get it?"

"From Aba Ben Mahoud."

"An Arab," McGuffin said, thinking aloud.

"He's some detective," Drumm said, jerking a thumb the detective's way.

McGuffin felt the urge to bend it back until it touched his elbow, but he fought it. Maybe later. "Where can I find Mahoud?"

"Just drive up Bel Air mountain, he's the sheik at the peak," the agent informed him, with a quick flash of her white teeth.

"I'd love to be there when you try to get in," Drumm said, with a satisfied smile. "He's got an Arab bodyguard who eats private detectives for breakfast."

"Then I'll go after feeding time," McGuffin answered.

"Let me give you another bit of advice, detective," the actor said in a sudden, angry whisper. "If you ever lay your hands on me again like you did just now, I'll save that Arab the trouble."

"Mark!" his agent warned sharply.

The actor squirmed but was immediately quiet. What McGuffin had heard was apparently true—in Hollywood the power lay with the agent.

"Did Mahoud make any money on Volper's pictures?" McGuffin asked Sloan, ignoring the sulking actor.

Her laugh was explosive. "My dear, in Hollywood the investor doesn't get paid back until the film recoups its original investment—which is almost never. I don't think *Gone With the Wind* has paid back its original investment yet."

"How much did he lose with Volper?" McGuffin asked.

She shrugged. "Several million—two or three each picture."

"And he kept coming back for more?"

"Nobody said he was a smart Arab," Drumm answered, lifting his bottle to his lips.

"Apparently," McGuffin mumbled, thinking that several million dollars was a more than adequate motive for murder, even for an Arab sheik. Bodyguard notwithstanding, he would somehow have to have a talk with Aba Ben Mahoud. "Will you get me an appointment with Mahoud?" he asked Judy Sloan.

"Not a chance, darling," she answered. "Mahoud was Ben's patsy. I've never even so much as spoken to him on the phone."

"Then how did Volper get in touch with him?"

"He didn't. Mahoud contacted him."

"He was a great admirer of Ben's first picture, *Fields of Flesh*," the actor put in.

"The one that made you a star," McGuffin observed. The actor only shrugged. "And I understand that picture had a lot to do with your success too," McGuffin said, looking at Judy Sloan.

"It can't hurt an agent to package a classic," she said, in a voice that sounded strangely like a hoarse purr.

"But it's been rather a long time since either of you has had another *Fields of Flesh*, hasn't it?" McGuffin said.

"I have clients other than Ben," she replied curtly.

"Like Mark?" McGuffin asked, thrusting a thumb in the actor's direction. "How long has it been since he made a picture? A few more like him and you'll be eligible for relief."

"Okay, that's it," Drumm said, pushing at McGuffin. "Get up, we're going out to the parking lot."

"You better call off your dog, lady," McGuffin warned softly.

Judy Sloan glanced nervously around the room to see who might be observing the belligerent behavior of her star, then smiled sweetly, like the mechanical shark in Jaws. "He's right, Mark," she whispered in a cheery singsong voice. "Shut your fucking mouth."

Reluctantly, Marvin Dumbrowski from the Bronx settled back in his banquette one more time. McGuffin, a keen judge of horseflesh, realized that Drumm had come to the end of his rope. One more insult and he would erupt, and this was plainly to be avoided. For besides the fact that Mark Drumm was big and well conditioned, he had the unmistakable aura of the volatile street fighter who, once aroused, would never stop coming of his own accord. McGuffin was glad Judy Sloan was along.

"A minute ago you told me that right now Mark Drumm is a hot property," McGuffin reminded her.

"I also told you that has nothing to do with Ben's disappearance."

"Come on," McGuffin urged. "Now that Volper may be dead, are you going to tell me there's no new interest in his work? Especially his first picture, *Fields of Flesh*? The picture that made Mark Drumm a star?"

"Naturally there's some interest," she admitted, waving her long brown cigarette carelessly in the air.

"There's more than interest," McGuffin said, deciding on a bluff. "I've heard that *Fields of Flesh* is going to be re-released."

"Who told you that?" Drumm demanded.

McGuffin ignored him. "Isn't that true?"

"There's been some talk, that's all," Judy Sloan hedged. "In Hollywood, talk is cheap."

"And life?" McGuffin asked.

"I don't get you," she said, fixing McGuffin with a feigned, patient smile.

"This is just hypothetical, you understand," McGuffin began, with a nod to Drumm. "In Hollywood, do you think a declining movie star would kill a producer just to revive his career?"

"No, but he might kill a detective if he ever got him alone," Drumm replied, in a flat, menacing voice.

"Mark!" Judy Sloan again warned.

"He's goin' too far," Drumm protested, slipping into his Bronx accent for the first time.

"When did you last see Ben Volper?" McGuffin demanded suddenly.

"Last week," Judy Sloan snapped back.

"You weren't at his house last Sunday, the day he disappeared?"

"We were there, but Ben wasn't," Drumm answered. "He was out walking on the beach when we arrived."

"Then Jenny discovered the suicide note in the typewriter and we went out looking for him," Judy added.

"And found his clothes," Drumm concluded, taking a last swig of beer.

"At what time?"

"A little after ten," Judy answered.

"Isn't that a little early?" McGuffin asked.

"You from New York?" she asked, eyeing McGuffin's tweed suit curiously.

"San Francisco."

"That explains it," she remarked.

"Explains what?"

"People from foreign climes—and to an Angeleno, San Francisco is as foreign as you can get—think Hollywood is a wild and crazy place, when in fact it's about as exciting as Levittown. Early to bed and early to rise."

Makes a man healthy, wealthy, and wise, McGuffin replied to himself. But in Ben Volper's case it was perhaps two out of three at best.

"Anyway, we always get there about ten," Judy Sloan

went on. "And Jenny discovered the note a little while after we'd all arrived."

"Who's we?" McGuffin demanded.

"Mark, me, David Hochman, and Isaac Stein—the Bronx Social Club," she said.

"The Bronx Social Club?" McGuffin repeated.

"It's a joke," she explained. "We're all from the same neighborhood."

"So I heard," McGuffin mumbled. "Then Ben's wife was the only one who saw him on the day he disappeared?"

"Apparently," Judy Sloan said. "You'd better ask her."

"Where can I find her?" McGuffin asked, making a squeaking noise as he slid to the edge of the banquette.

"At the Colony," Mark Drumm answered, signaling for another beer.

"The Colony?" McGuffin asked, climbing to his feet.

"The *Malibu* Colony," Drumm replied, sliding his dark glasses down his nose.

"Oh, that colony," McGuffin said, looking closely at Mark Drumm's eyes. The actor, he could now see, was stoned. He thanked them, started to go, then stopped. "If I have any more questions, I hope you'll be easier to get to the next time."

"I'm always easy, Mr. McGuffin," Judy Sloan assured him.

3

McGuffin hurried out of the Polo Lounge and through the lobby, calling his name to the car attendant as he skipped down the broad stairs. A few minutes later his car nosed over the top of the drive and came to rest in front of the hotel.

Unable to find anything smaller than a five-dollar bill, McGuffin regretfully handed it over to the blond, blue-eyed attendant, an aspiring actor, no doubt, and slid under the wheel. The attendant accepted the bill with neither shame nor surprise, then closed the door on his benefactor.

"How do I get to the Malibu Colony?" McGuffin asked.

"Straight out Sunset, up the Pacific Coast Highway, across the road from the Malibu shopping center—you can't miss it," he assured him.

McGuffin knew better. "Thanks," he said, as he put the car into a long glide down the drive to Sunset Boulevard.

"Sunset Boulevard," he whispered to himself, as he proceeded west in the late afternoon sun, between rows of tall palm trees. Somewhere up one of these secret driveways is the house where William Holden discovered Norma Desmond, after thinking she had been dead for years. I should be so lucky with Ben Volper, he thought, slowing for still another sharp curve on the twisting boulevard. Driving was not one of the things he did best.

Ahead lay Pacific Palisades, the former home of a second-rate actor who had risen to become the President of the United States. McGuffin began to hum "Hooray for Hol-

lywood!" as he tapped his fingers to the rhythm on the
steering wheel of the Japanese car. A long, gentle slope at
the end of Sunset Boulevard emptied onto the Pacific Coast
Highway. With the crashing waves of the Pacific Ocean on
his left and the sun-baked foothills of the Topanga Moun-
tains on his right, McGuffin rushed to a rendezvous with
the glamorous Jenny Lang, once the most voluptuous woman
in Hollywood. He both wondered and dreaded what time
had done to that statuesque body, as he absently patted his
own paunch.

He found the shopping center and the Malibu Colony,
just as the parking attendant had promised, a modest en-
clave of stucco cottages resembling a Mexican village in
everything but price. There was one thing McGuffin hadn't
counted on—a gatekeeper.

He asked for McGuffin's name, then consulted his clip-
board.

"Sorry, Mrs. Volper didn't leave your name," he informed
McGuffin.

"Her father-in-law sent me. If you'll just phone her?"
McGuffin suggested.

"Sorry, I can't do that. If your name ain't on the list, you
can't get in. I don't make the rules," he said, turning his
back on McGuffin and returning to the guard shack.

Okay, McGuffin thought, as he backed the car and turned
it around. There's more than one way to see a star.

He drove back to the highway, turned in the direction
from which he had come and drove for about a mile to a
parking area above the beach. He nosed his car in among
the customized vans, got out, and walked to the edge of the
cliff. There were a couple of dozen surfers on the beach
below, girls in the tiniest of bikinis, boys in cut-off jeans,
all of them just one long, lean, sun-browned muscle. They
stared curiously at the middle-aged man in the tweed suit
as he climbed down the path to the beach.

"Hi, how's the surf?" McGuffin greeted as he walked
past them.

"Gnarly, Pop," one of them replied. He was older than
McGuffin would have expected of a surfer, with a Fu Man-

chu mustache and a blood-dripping dagger tattooed on one arm. "Where'd you get the wet suit?" he called after McGuffin, followed by flunky laughter.

McGuffin smiled, but kept walking. He wished he could stay around to watch them grow old.

The tide was out, but moving in, the lower part of the beach hard and the walking easy. When the first of the Colony houses came into view, he became careless, and a wave splashed over his shoes. He muttered and slapped his wet shoes angrily on the firm sand, then climbed to a softer but drier trail on the beach. It was hot and his tweed trousers were beginning to itch. Must get a summer suit if this case stretches out, he reminded himself. In San Francisco, only tourists wore light summer clothes. It was just one of the many differences between the two cities.

Drawing abreast of the row of houses, McGuffin suddenly realized that finding Volper's house might be more of a problem than he had anticipated. While the front of the house might be identified by a name, the rear, with its deck and obligatory hot tub, was no less anonymous than the facing sea. Several houses down, a Chicano maid in a starched white uniform was sweeping the deck.

McGuffin stopped and shouted: "Do you know where the Volper house is?"

She stared quietly for a moment—she didn't often see a shod man in a tweed suit walking the beach—then pointed up the beach. "Volpair, one, two, three house—way back!" she called, proud of her English.

"*Gracias, señora!*" McGuffin called, equally proud of his Spanish.

The Volper house was indeed way back from the others, behind a low dune with beach grass and purple flowers blowing in the wind. McGuffin climbed the few stairs to the narrow catwalk that led to the deck. The sliding-glass door was open and a diaphanous yellow curtain billowed out over the deck like an exotic kite. The solarium and hot tub would be behind the redwood fence to his right, McGuffin guessed. He wanted to peek over the fence, just on the chance Jenny Lang might be sunbathing in the nude, but he proceeded instead directly to the glass door.

His knock was answered almost instantly by a Chicano maid in a starched white uniform—they seemed to come with the property.

"No more newspaper, no more newspaper!" she exclaimed, shooing him away as she rushed across the room at him.

"I'm not with the newspapers," McGuffin protested, pushing his card at her.

Ignoring the card, she gathered the curtain and pulled it inside, as if she were a parachutist who had just dropped onto the deck, then began sliding the glass door closed on him.

"Just a minute!" McGuffin ordered, planting a foot firmly on the aluminum track.

Hardened perhaps by a lifetime of menial service, the maid hurtled the sliding door down the track with the speed of a Japanese train. McGuffin gasped at the sudden bone-crushing pain, then reached involuntarily for his trapped foot, banging his head on the glass.

"Dolores!" a female voice cried.

The door opened and McGuffin felt a hand on his arm.

"Are you all right?" a sweetly familiar Swedish voice trilled.

His head ringing, McGuffin looked up from a crouch at the face of Jenny Lang. The face was fuller than he had remembered and there were lines he had not seen before, but all the glorious colors were still intact: the thick, careless hair that billowed like clouds at sunset, the ripe peach complexion, the full dark lips, and the eyes, blue and clear as vodka and tonic.

"I'm fine," he gasped.

"Let me help you," she said, pulling him erect in spite of himself.

McGuffin leaned lightly on her, until his foot hit the floor. Then he grunted and fell heavily on her shoulder, limping down two stairs and skipping across the room on one foot. She was a big strong woman.

"Thank you," he said, sliding to the couch.

"Can I get you something?" she asked, hovering over him.

"An X-ray," he answered, as he rubbed his foot.

"Oh!" she exclaimed, bringing both hands to her face. "Do you think it's broken?"

"No, it's all right," McGuffin quickly assured her. Seeing the frightened look on her face, he instantly regretted his little joke.

"Are you sure? Shall I call a doctor?"

"I'm fine," he insisted. "Really, the pain is almost all gone."

"Thank heavens!" she exclaimed, straightening up with a great sigh.

Her breasts loomed above McGuffin like a great bank of rain clouds. She was, he decided then and there, still the most voluptuous woman in Hollywood. She wore a blue denim shirt knotted under her breasts, khaki shorts, and monk's sandals. McGuffin was amazed—even after all these years she looked very nearly the same as she had on the silver screen.

"Dolores is so protective since my husband's disappearance," Mrs. Volper explained.

"I understand," McGuffin said, reaching into his jacket for another card. The first one was blowing down the beach.

"Amos McGuffin—private investigator?" she read.

"Your father-in-law hired me."

"Oh, yes," she remembered. "He phoned." She turned to the maid and smiled. "Thank you, Dolores, you can go."

Glowering but obedient, Dolores backed reluctantly out of the room, as her mistress sat on the ottoman opposite McGuffin, pressing her long suntanned legs together. McGuffin stared at her with a faint, satisfied grin, of which he was scarcely aware.

"Is there nothing you would like?" she asked hesitantly.

"No, no, nothing," McGuffin said, quickly shaking the grin from his face. He would have liked to go on staring at her for the rest of the day, but that, he knew, would scarcely inspire her confidence. "I'd just like to ask a few questions."

She nodded once and waited, hands laced tightly across her

knees. "I hate to be blunt about this, Mrs. Volper—Do you prefer Mrs. Volper, or Miss Lang?"

"Mrs. Volper," she answered.

"Well, the fact is—I don't think Mr. Volper has disappeared. I think he's staged his disappearance just to get publicity for his new picture."

"Do you?" she asked, squirming with excitement, as if this were new to her.

McGuffin smiled. "You aren't putting me on, are you, Mrs. Volper?"

"Putting you on?" she repeated.

"Because this is costing Mr. Volpersky a lot of money— not to mention mental anguish. So if you know where your husband is hiding, why don't you tell me and I'll tell Mr. Volpersky and that'll be the end of it," he coaxed.

Her clear blue eyes sought out McGuffin's and held. "Mr. McGuffin," she said patiently, "if I knew where Ben was, I would have told his father."

"Hmm," McGuffin said softly, shaking his head slowly. "Then you give me your word this is not a publicity stunt?"

"I will give you my word on that," she said firmly.

"Damn," McGuffin muttered. He was expecting a piece of cake. He got to his feet and limped across the room to the now closed glass door. She might lie to strangers, but it was hard to believe she would allow her father-in-law to dangle unnecessarily in the wind. Nor could he believe that any sane man would check out on a woman like Jenny Lang Volper. Or all this, he thought, turning his back to the sea. The large room was expensively furnished with masculine things—a bar, a leather chesterfield and an Eames chair along with an eclectic display of handsome antiques. The wall facing him was lined with mahogany shelves, stuffed with books that looked to have been read and curious trinkets, remembrances of good times. The house even had its own movie projection booth jutting out from the wall to the right at the far end of the room, although that was scarcely a luxury in Malibu, McGuffin knew. He limped back across the room and dropped heavily onto the couch opposite her.

"Mr. Volpersky doesn't think his son is a candidate for

suicide," McGuffin informed her. "What do you think?"

She unlaced her hands and let them fly. "I don't know." She sighed. She looked at the floor for a moment, then raised her face to McGuffin. It was a sad and confused face. "You don't like to think such a thing," she said softly.

"But there is a possibility?" he asked, equally soft.

She stared at him and bit her lower lip, unable or afraid to answer. It was apparent that she had either asked herself this question many times lately and didn't like the answer, or had until now managed to avoid it.

"I'm sorry, Mrs. Volper, but I have to know," McGuffin said.

She nodded. "I understand." Now *she* got to her feet and walked across the room to take McGuffin's place, staring out to sea. When she finally spoke, she did not look at McGuffin. "It's very difficult," she began. "But I know I must answer these questions sooner or later, if only to myself."

She turned to her left and walked slowly toward the projection booth on the opposite wall, head bowed, like a monk at prayer. Her voice came in short soft bursts. "I blame myself. For not having taken things seriously. But it isn't easy to admit such things. You tell yourself they will go away." She stopped at the wall and stared silently at the tiny rectangular opening in the projection booth.

"What things, Mrs. Volper?" McGuffin prodded gently.

"Something was bothering him," she said, turning and starting slowly back across the room. "I can see that now. Ben had changed."

"How?" McGuffin asked.

She stopped in the middle of the room. "He distrusted people. He thought everyone was trying to use him. One by one, he cut off all his friends, until there were only a few."

"The Bronx Social Club?"

"You know about them?" she asked, glancing quickly at McGuffin.

McGuffin nodded. "I just came from a meeting with Judy Sloan and Mark Drumm."

"It's very hard on them," she said. "They were such close friends. Especially Mark. Ben is like his older brother."

That wasn't McGuffin's reading, but he saw no reason to disillusion her. Instead he observed: "Mark Drumm seems to have a rather short fuse."

"Short fuse—I don't know what this means," she said with a helpless shrug.

"Sorry. He looks like he could be violent."

"Oh, not anymore, I am sure," she said dismissively. "That was only when he was younger."

"What was when he was younger?"

"Well, he—he used to get in fights—in bars," she explained, somewhat reluctantly, McGuffin thought. "But since he stopped drinking, he doesn't do that anymore."

"What about cocaine?" McGuffin asked. "Does he do much coke?"

"Not much, I don't think," she replied. 'In Hollywood most everyone does a little, I'm afraid."

"Your husband?"

"Rarely, if ever."

He wanted to ask the actress if she did, but he knew it was none of his business. It also wasn't very likely, he was somehow sure. She returned to the ottoman, sat, and looked into McGuffin's eyes with a deep concern that fairly caused his heart to dance.

"How is your foot?" she inquired gravely.

"Fine, fine," he assured her. "It sounds as if your husband was a bit paranoid," McGuffin suggested.

"I wasn't able to admit this at the time, but I'm afraid you are right," she answered, looking away from him.

"Enough to kill himself?"

When she absently twirled her hair, McGuffin had a strange feeling of déjà vu—until he remembered. It was a familiar acting gesture, from *Fields of Flesh*. Was she acting now? he suddenly wondered. Or was it a natural gesture that had only inadvertently crept into her screen performance?

"I'm afraid so," she answered, then sighed, perhaps relieved.

"What about the rest of the Bronx Social Club, Isaac Stein and David Hochman?" he asked. "Were they equally friendly with your husband?"

"Yes, I would have to say—they were the only real friends he had, the only people he trusted," she answered.

"And you? What did he feel for you?"

She was slow to answer. "I thought our marriage was good. But—he didn't confide in me, did he?" She bit her lip and looked away. "I think there were maybe two Ben Volpers," she said softly after a moment. "The one I married and the one who did this."

"I'm sorry," McGuffin said. "I came down here thinking this was something else." When he bumped his foot against the ottoman, he winced involuntarily.

"Your foot is hurting you, isn't it?" she asked.

"It'll be fine," he said, enjoying her concern. "Why don't you tell me what happened last Sunday?"

"Yes, last Sunday," she repeated with a faraway look. "I knew something was troubling Ben, but he wouldn't tell me what it was. He wouldn't talk. He avoided me all morning. Then he went out for a walk and didn't come back," she said, with a puzzled look.

McGuffin pressed for details, but got little more than he had already heard from Judy Sloan and Mark Drumm. Volper had gone out shortly before the Bronx Social Club began arriving at ten, and Jenny had discovered the unsigned suicide note in his typewriter a short while later.

"Could anyone other than your husband have left that note without your knowing it?" he asked.

"I don't see how," she answered. "You don't seriously think someone could have—" She couldn't finish the sentence.

"Do you?" McGuffin asked. "He's a powerful man, surely he has some enemies."

"Not that sort," she said with certainty.

"I understand his films lost a lot of money for a man named Aba Ben Mahoud."

"You have met Mahoud?" she asked.

"Not yet. Have you?"

"Only once, with Ben. He's extremely wealthy. The money he lost with Ben meant nothing to him."

"Is Aba Ben Mahoud the sort of man who could kill?" McGuffin asked.

"Oh, I don't think so!" she replied, with a wide-eyed expression.

"How can I get in touch with him?"

"I don't know." She shrugged. "Whenever Ben wanted to get in touch with him, he had to leave a message with a friend, but I don't know who this friend is. I'm sorry."

"That's all right, I'll find him," McGuffin promised. Getting into tight places like the Malibu Colony was his specialty.

"Tell me about *Fields of Flesh*," McGuffin said. "That was Mark Drumm's first big picture, wasn't it?"

"Yes." She nodded. "And Isaac's and David's."

"The whole Bronx Social Club?"

"Except for me. I am the Swedish shiksa," she said, with a laugh that felt to McGuffin like a massage. If she had killed her husband, it would be very hard for McGuffin to bring her in.

"Did Drumm make any other pictures with your husband?"

She shook her head. "After *Fields of Flesh* Mark's price went to over a million dollars—Ben could no longer afford him."

"But he hasn't worked much lately."

"Nevertheless, he won't reduce his fee. It's silly, but that's the way it is in Hollywood."

"You sound as if you don't consider yourself a part of it," McGuffin observed.

"I retired undefeated. See?" she said, pointing to her eyes. "No scar tissue." Her smile was like a field of flowers.

"And no regrets?" he asked.

"None. I have enough money; I have a full life; I do volunteer work. The only thing I don't have," she said, pressing her hands tightly together, "is my husband."

"I'll do what I can to find him," McGuffin said, getting to his feet. He stepped on his injured foot without pain, then remembered. "Do you suppose I might lean on you—just as far as the deck?"

"Of course," she said, jumping up to help him. She placed his arm over her shoulder and her own around his waist. "Promise me you'll see a doctor," she said, as she helped him across the room."

"Uh-huh," McGuffin said, again with the vague, satisfied grin.

"Where is your car?" she asked, when they were standing on the edge of the deck, nothing but sand and ocean ahead of them.

"Down the beach. Don't worry, I'll manage," he assured her.

She looked doubtful as she released him.

"Do you mind if I ask you a personal question?" McGuffin said.

"I'll let you know after you ask," she replied, with another dazzling smile.

"How much is a house like this worth?"

She laughed. "I don't know," she answered with an unconcerned shrug. "Perhaps five million dollars?"

McGuffin whistled. "Five million. It must be the view. Not that it isn't a nice house," he added quickly. Like most San Franciscans, McGuffin seldom even looked at the ocean. To him it was something that made it difficult to get from one continent to another. "It must make you nervous," he commented.

"What?"

"The ocean. Don't these houses get washed out once in a while?" he asked, remembering newspaper pictures of movie stars sandbagging their houses during a storm.

"Not this one," she said, smiling confidently. "This one is farther back than the others, and we have that big dune to protect us.

"I'm glad of that," McGuffin said. "Five million would be a lot to pay for a leaky houseboat."

Her laugh made him weak.

He limped down the beach until he was safely out of her sight, then he began to jog. Seeing Jenny Lang so little changed over the years filled him with energy. Several hundred yards down the beach, however, he pulled up with a stitch in his side. Next week, he promised himself, I start working out.

The surfers were still huddled together on the beach under the cliff when McGuffin returned. The one with the Fu Manchu mustache mumbled something to the others, setting off a giggle, when he saw McGuffin. McGuffin passed wordlessly and hauled himself up the cliff.

When he got to the top, he saw what they'd been giggling about. All four tires on the Toyota were flat.

"Shit," he muttered.

"Looks like you got trouble, Pop."

McGuffin turned. Fu Manchu stood near the top of the path, his grinning flunkies fanned out behind him.

"Yeah, it does look that way," McGuffin agreed, placing his hands wearily on the trunk lid.

"Them Jap tires never did hold air worth a shit," Fu Manchu remarked, as he approached arrogantly.

McGuffin studied them. They were mean kids with nothing to lose. "That's okay," McGuffin said, reaching into his pants pocket. "I've got something here that'll take care of it."

"Watcha got there?" the surfer asked, as McGuffin inserted the key in the trunk lid. "A pump? 'Cuz a pump won't do much against an ice-pick hole," he said, turning to the crowd for a laugh.

"No, I don't have a pump," McGuffin said, unzipping a duffel bag. It was empty except for a lead statue of the Virgin, about two feet high.

"Watcha gonna do, Pop, pray?" he asked, when McGuffin brought the statue out.

"No, I'm not gonna pray," he said, removing a panel from the base of the statue. He dropped the panel into the duffel bag and slid his hand into the statue. "And this isn't a pump, it's a Smith and Wesson nine-millimeter automatic," he said, removing a shiny gray gun from the statue. "And it's a hell of a lot more effective than an ice pick."

"Hey, Pop, wait a minute!" the surfer implored, showing

his empty hands. "It was just a little joke; we'll take care of the tires!"

"Which one of these vans is yours?" McGuffin asked, waving the gun in the direction of the parked vehicles.

"Whataya mean? I ain't got no van."

McGuffin gripped the gun in both hands and aimed it directly at Fu Manchu's mustache.

"That one!" He pointed to a shiny red one with turret windows and an ocean sunset painted on the side.

"Whatcha gonna do?"

McGuffin walked over to the van, pointed the gun at the rear tire, and fired. The tire exploded and one corner of the van settled heavily on the hard sand.

"Oh, man!" the surfer moaned nasally.

McGuffin moved to the other wheel and fired again. Then twice more until the van was resting on four rims. Finished, he returned to the Toyota, dropped his few things into the duffel bag, then turned and walked to the highway. He phoned for a cab at the drugstore in the Malibu shopping center, then placed a second call to the Executive Rent-A-Car company.

"Disabled vehicle across from Malibu shopping center," the woman from Executive repeated. She had no wish to know how the car had become disabled. "We'll have another car at the Beverly Hills Hotel within the hour," she said.

When the cab driver dropped McGuffin in front of the hotel, another car was waiting. He made a mental note to write a congratulatory letter to the president of Executive Rent-A-Car.

That night, McGuffin had dinner at the Polo Lounge. Sadly, he sipped Calistoga water while gazing longingly at the drinks passing back and forth between the bar and his table. If I can get through this, he told himself, I'll know I'm not an alcoholic.

He passed the test, then wandered around the hotel, listening to the tinkle of cocktail glasses, coming to rest finally in front of the newsstand. He would buy a book and return to the bungalow, out of alcohol's way. He thumbed through the paperbacks, rejecting the best-sellers as too long for a one-night read, and settled on a detective story. They amused him because they were so much more exciting than the real thing. After all, he thought, starting back to his bungalow with his book tucked under his arm, who'd want to read a story about a private eye who goes looking for the body of a suicide victim?

Before getting into bed, he phoned David Hochman for the second time that evening, but again got only his machine. He hung up without leaving a message and climbed into bed with his book.

He figured out who did it on page 148, then changed his mind fifty pages later. A few pages after that he decided he didn't care one way or the other who did it, so he tossed the book across the room and tried David Hochman one more time. Again he wasn't home. This time he left a message.

If this were a detective novel, I'd get dressed and go to Hochman's house and find him dead in the bathtub with a mysterious message scrawled on the tile in his own blood.

"But it's not," he murmured, as he fluffed up the pillow and went promptly to sleep.

McGuffin was awakened by the phone the next morning. He pulled his arm out from under the pillow and glanced at his watch as he reached for the receiver. It was only nine o'clock. Kind of early for a Hollywood writer, it seemed.

"Hello?"

"Mr. McGuffin?" a male voice inquired.

"Mr. Hochman?"

"No, this is not Mr. Hochman," the caller replied starchily. "This is Mr. Worthy of Executive Rent-A-Car."

"Oh, yeah, the flat tires." McGuffin yawned.

"Flat tires!" Worthy squeaked. "Your car, Mr. McGuffin, was found in the Pacific Ocean, beaten into a small ball of steel!"

"Really?" McGuffin asked, sitting up in bed.

"That's right, Mr. McGuffin. And before I turn this matter over to our attorneys, I would like some explanation."

"Fu Manchu," McGuffin thought aloud.

"Pardon me?"

"Surfers," McGuffin explained. "They did it."

"Surfers," Worthy repeated. "You mean kids on surfboards."

"That's right," McGuffin replied. "Only one of them is a little long in the tooth. The one with the Fu Manchu mustache and the dagger tattoo. Find him and you've got your man."

"A surfer with a Fu Manchu mustache and a dagger tattoo," Mr. Worthy said slowly, as if speaking a foreign phrase.

"That's him."

"You actually saw him destroy our car and push it into the ocean?"

"No, but it's a reasonable presumption," McGuffin assured him. "You see, one of them let the air out of my tires, so I let the air out of his tires—although not exactly in the same way—and then I left. That's when they must have wrecked the car and pushed it into the ocean."

"So it would seem," Worthy mumbled. "Would you mind telling me why you didn't stay with the car?"

"Are you kidding?" McGuffin asked. "You think I wanted to get beat up and dumped in the ocean?"

"I think there's more to this than what you're telling me," Worthy said.

"Mr. Worthy!" McGuffin exclaimed in a wounded tone. "You aren't implying that I'm lying, are you?"

"I'm not implying, Mr. McGuffin. I'll leave it to our lawyers to get to the bottom of it. But I'm putting you on notice, do not ever again attempt to rent a car from Executive Rent-A-Car."

"Well, I guess I won't," McGuffin replied haughtily, as the phone went dead in his ear. "And to think I was going to write him a congratulatory letter," he muttered as he threw back the blanket and fairly sprang out of bed. Halfway across the room, he stopped. Something was vaguely wrong, but he didn't know what it was. Then he remembered. He had no hangover.

4

David Hochman's house was on a broad palm-lined street in Beverly Hills, a large colonial with a white Rolls-Royce parked at the front door, not much different from any of the other houses on the block. McGuffin left his rented Toyota at the curb and walked across the springy manicured lawn to the columned stoop.

The door was answered by a bearded suntanned man in jeans and work shirt, the gardener, McGuffin supposed.

"Yes?" he inquired, curiously regarding McGuffin's tweed suit.

"I'd like to see your boss," McGuffin said, pulling a card from his shirt pocket.

"Sorry, I'm freelance," the man replied, plucking a pair of tortoiseshell glasses from the top of his head.

"You're David Hochman?"

"Absolutely," he said, studying McGuffin's card through his glasses. "McGuffin—is that really your name?"

"Absolutely," McGuffin answered.

"How very droll," he said, returning the card to McGuffin. "You're here about poor Ben, of course. Come in." He motioned to his guest.

"Thanks," McGuffin said, and stepped inside. "I guess I hadn't expected a Hollywood writer to answer his own door."

"I can't have servants in the house while I'm working," the writer explained. "I'm in the study," he said, leading McGuffin through the wide center hall to the French doors opening onto the patio.

The walls were covered with oil portraits of David Hochman, his wife, and kids. McGuffin stopped at the last portrait—something was wrong.

"They're different wives," Hochman said. "I've had five, and eleven children. It's a form of discipline. If I didn't have the expense, I couldn't write this shlock." The last portrait was a framed blank canvas. "I'm engaged," the writer explained and stepped through the French doors.

McGuffin followed, setting off a terrible howl. When he lifted his foot, a cat dashed into the house, meowing furiously. "Sorry," McGuffin apologized.

"It's all right, I have plenty," the writer said.

And indeed, there were a great number of cats napping around the pool, as well as a large desk, sheltered by a fringed umbrella.

"Your study?" McGuffin asked.

The writer nodded. "This is where the deathless prose is composed," he said, indicating a chair beside the desk.

McGuffin sat, while the writer perched himself on the corner of his desk.

"Aren't you a little hot in that suit?" Hochman asked.

"A little," McGuffin allowed, slipping his jacket off. There were large, damp patches under both arms.

"So how are things in New York?" Hochman asked.

McGuffin shrugged. "Fine, I suppose."

"You suppose?"

"I'm from San Francisco."

The writer was puzzled. "Ben disappears in Los Angeles and his father in New York hires a San Francisco detective?"

"How do you know Ben's father hired me?" McGuffin asked.

He shrugged. "Judy Sloan mentioned it, I guess. She's my agent."

"Apparently Judy Sloan represents the entire Bronx Social Club," McGuffin observed.

Hochman winked. "Gotta keep it in the family." He pushed a pile of papers aside and slid back on the desk, letting his feet swing freely, like a kid fishing from a bridge. In spite of the gray-streaked beard, his face had a mischievous, boyish look. There were two wireless telephones and a computer on the desk, along with a pile of newspapers and a pair of scissors. All the newspapers were cut up and the snipped articles (possible movie ideas, McGuffin guessed) were piled high in a basket atop the desk.

"No typewriter?" McGuffin observed.

"Typewriter!" Hochman exclaimed. "Why not a quill pen, or a Gutenberg press? This," he said, stroking the screened computer atop his desk, as if it were a prized cat, "is the writing instrument of the twenty-first century—the word processor! One simply fills the machine with plots and characters, then importunes it for a shooting script—comedy, tragedy, comical-tragedy, tragical-comedy—whatever the public is buying. Or at least that's the way the producers seem to think it's done," he muttered, reaching across the desk for a cigarette.

David Hochman, McGuffin decided, was not a contented writer. "I take it you don't like producers," he observed.

"Aha!" the writer exclaimed, holding a cigarette aloft, as if it were a piece of chalk. "The quick-witted detective closes in for the kill! 'I hated him,' the suspect admits. 'Enough to kill him?' the gumshoe snarls. 'I didn't say that.' The suspect squirms, beads of sweat breaking out on his forehead.

"No, Mr. McGuffin," he said, flipping the cigarette in the air and catching it in his mouth, "I didn't dislike Ben Volper. I loved him like a brother."

"Then you think he's dead."

"It's hard to think anything else, isn't it?" he asked. He lit his cigarette and tossed the match over his shoulder into the pool. There were, McGuffin noticed, a great number of cigarette butts and matches floating on the water. "To me it's just a million-dollar ashtray," the writer explained, noticing McGuffin's interest. "Can't swim a stroke. Where I grew up in the Bronx, the waterfront was in Italian territory."

"Do you know any reason Volper might have wanted to commit suicide?" McGuffin asked.

"The same reason we all have," Hochman answered. "You

come out here expecting to do great things, but you just keep sliding deeper and deeper into shit. You can either lie there and roll around in it, or you can do what Ben did. You can go into the ocean and get clean."

McGuffin shook his head. He couldn't believe a man committed suicide because he didn't like his job. "It seems to pay well enough," he observed, with a nod to the house.

"The lower you sink, the more you make," Hochman answered.

"Did you make a lot with Ben Volper?"

"A bit. I wrote *Fields of Flesh* with Ben."

"Did you do his last one?"

"*Lemmings*? No, that was written by an episodic."

"Episodic?"

"An episodic is someone who writes series television," the writer explained.

"Sounds like a disease."

"Out here it is," Hochman said, drawing deeply on his cigarette.

"Do you ever do episodic?"

The writer nodded. "When you got five wives and eleven kids, you do what you have to do."

"When did you last work for Ben Volper?"

"Several years ago. But we were working on a script when he died," the writer quickly added.

"What'll happen to it now?" McGuffin asked.

"I'll sell it to somebody else. Ben didn't need me and I didn't need him. That was the secret of our friendship, Mr. McGuffin," the writer assured him.

"That's what Ben's father said."

"Must be tough on the old man," Hochman said, and flipped his cigarette into the pool. It landed with a quick hiss that woke the cat sleeping nearby.

"It's going to be a lot worse if I have to report that his son killed himself."

Hochman gestured helplessly. "What else can it be?"

"A hoax?"

Hochman shook his head. "Ben would never put his father through something like that."

"Unless he had suddenly become insane," McGuffin qualified.

"Who said that?" the writer demanded.

"Do you deny that Ben Volper was a paranoid?" McGuffin asked, confident that sooner or later, one of Volper's friends would confirm what his wife had only hinted.

"He wasn't paranoid," Hochman replied, with little conviction. "He had a few minor episodes, that was all."

"Apparently the last one was major," McGuffin said.

Hochman shook his head. "I can't believe that. Not Ben."

"Did you see him on the day he disappeared?" McGuffin asked.

"No," Hochman admitted. "Only Jenny saw him."

McGuffin got to his feet. It wasn't a happy ending, but it looked as if the Ben Volper case was rapidly drawing to a close. "I'm staying at the Beverly Hills Hotel. Give me a call if you think of anything, will you?" McGuffin asked.

"The Beverly Hills?" the writer said, sliding off the desk. "Whatever happened to the old fifty a day plus expenses?"

"Gone the way of the ten-cent subway fare," McGuffin answered.

Hochman laughed and clapped a hand on McGuffin's shoulder. "You're okay, McGuffin."

"Thanks," McGuffin said.

"If there's anything I can do, just let me know," he said, as he led McGuffin back through the house.

"Can you put me in touch with the director Isaac Stein?"

"It's done," Hochman assured him. "Zak's shooting a weekly at MGM. I'll have a pass waiting for you at the gate when you get there."

McGuffin thanked him again and asked: "Is a weekly anything like an episodic?"

"Movie of the week—it's one step up," he answered.

At the door they shook hands. David Hochman was slow to release his grip, and, for a moment, McGuffin had the feeling there was something more the writer wanted to tell him.

"Tell me, Amos—can I call you Amos?"

"Sure."

"And you call me David." McGuffin nodded and waited. "Tell me, Amos, in your business you must come across a lot of interesting stories, right?"

"Some," McGuffin allowed, feeling the pressure on his hand tighten.

"Anything," he asked, squeezing tighter, "that might make a good movie?"

Shit, McGuffin said to himself, as he wrestled the writer for his hand. "If I think of anything I'll let you know," he promised, as he stepped off the porch.

"NBC is looking for a detective series," the writer went on, as he hurried after McGuffin. "I got a lot of plot ideas, I just need a character, something like a hook. Like a guy who wears tweed suits in L.A. That's it!" he exclaimed. "Amos! Amos!"

McGuffin began to trot, but the writer stayed with him across the lawn and to the car. McGuffin slammed the door shut and started the engine.

"We'll split fifty-fifty!" the writer called through the glass.

McGuffin pulled away with a squeak of rubber, leaving David Hochman an image in the rearview mirror.

"Make it sixty-forty!" the writer called.

5

McGuffin parked his car in the lot in front of the Metro-Goldwyn-Mayer office building and walked to the fabled MGM gate. As Hochman had promised, and to McGuffin's surprise (things seldom went so well for him), there was a pass waiting for him at the gate. The guard gave him directions to the *Stakeout in Watts* set, and McGuffin, mindful of all the movie detectives who had passed this way before him, especially the great Bogart, walked onto the MGM lot. He had never been on a studio lot before, but he had seen movies of them, bustling with stagehands, cowboys, and harem girls, and a famous star gliding by in a long convertible, so he knew what to expect. However, before he had gone very far, one more of an ever-dwindling supply of youthful fantasies was forever lost.

The narrow asphalt streets between the big frame buildings were very nearly deserted. Thirty years ago there would have been a movie being shot on every sound stage on the lot, but today, not a QUIET sign hung from a single door. Today's movies were being made "on location" by independent producers, and each picture cost many times more than all of Cagney's back-lot classics combined. All the Hawks and Fords were gone now, replaced by the biz-school guys, who, although they believed firmly in a diversified stock portfolio for themselves, were willing to hock the studio on the chance of a single blockbuster movie. If the gamble paid off, the studio head was a genius; if it didn't he was an agent. Something was definitely ailing the movie industry, but McGuffin didn't have time to diagnose it. He had enough to do just trying to find one missing producer.

When he passed an open second-story door off a long catwalk, he heard the lonely sound of one typewriter clacking. Next year's blockbuster, McGuffin mused, as he rounded the corner of the yellow barrackslike building. When he saw the sign on the building, MEDICAL OFFICE, he realized that it was not the great American film script being typed, but probably an insurance form.

McGuffin was beginning to think he was lost until, at the end of a narrow alley, he caught sight of a film crew. That must be they, he decided, slipping between the yellow frame buildings. For all the glamour of the industry, a movie lot looked not much different from an army post.

As he stepped out into the street, one of the film crew pointed and shouted, but McGuffin couldn't hear him over the screech of tires. He looked to his right, saw a car fishtailing wildly toward him, and dived back into the alley as the car skidded past, missing him by inches, before bouncing off a building and sliding toward the film crew. They scattered in all directions as the car plowed forward into the lights and camera, hurtling pieces of equipment into the air before coming finally to rest.

A tall hawk-nosed man in a New York Yankees baseball jersey rushed to help the driver out of the car. Apparently unhurt, the driver climbed out from under the wheel, while the rest of the film crew, like survivors of a hurricane, returned slowly to the carnage. The man in the baseball jersey inquired anxiously after the well-being of each. Then, satisfied that no one was injured, he sadly regarded the camera, shattered on the ground, spewing film that looked like torn guts. He stared at it as if it were a dead child and shook his head sadly. Lying near the camera, McGuffin saw when he got closer, was a chalkboard inscribed STAKEOUT IN WATTS, ISAAC STEIN, DIREC.

"Oh shit," McGuffin mumbled.

Isaac Stein turned, viewfinder swinging from his neck, and studied McGuffin, much as a pitcher might study a dangerous batter.

"Sorry," McGuffin apologized, throwing in a quick smile. "I didn't know you were shooting a movie here."

"And what did you think we'd be doing on a movie lot?" he asked, in a voice seething with restraint. "Harvesting pineapples?"

"Sorry," McGuffin mumbled again. "But at least nobody got hurt," he added brightly, as if injury were the usual effect of his visits.

"No, nobody got hurt," the director admitted, with a too-friendly smile. "You've destroyed a camera and half a day's work, but nobody was hurt. Now would you mind leaving before somebody does get hurt," he ordered, pointing in the direction McGuffin had just come.

"Right away," McGuffin promised, producing his card.

The director looked at it, then at McGuffin. "You're the guy Dave phoned about? The guy who's supposed to find Ben?" McGuffin nodded. The director shook his head slowly, as if shaking off the catcher's sign. "Bad casting," he said. Then he turned to the crew and ordered them to break for lunch. He told his young assistant to clean up the mess and see about a new camera.

"What do I tell production?" the assistant director asked, staring at the broken camera.

"Wear and tear," the director said, as he turned and walked away from the mess, followed by McGuffin.

They walked silently in the direction McGuffin had come to one of the large frame buildings he had passed, up the exterior stairs, and down the catwalk to an open door. Inside, an attractive young woman in jeans and T-shirt, feet up on the desk, sat reading *Rolling Stone*. She didn't look up when Isaac Stein stopped at the desk to leaf through the mail.

"If anybody calls, I'm not here," he said, dropping the mail on the desk.

"Uh-huh," she answered, turning the page, as McGuffin followed the director into the next office.

The director of a weekly was apparently not a force to be reckoned with, McGuffin noted.

Stein closed the door and McGuffin sat on the couch in front of the window. The walls were hung with forties movie posters and the shelves were stuffed with movie scripts. Stein plopped heavily in the chair behind his desk, rubbed his eyes, and stared curiously at McGuffin for a moment.

"Please be careful of the vase," he said, pointing.

McGuffin's elbow nicked the vase on the end table as he turned, but he snatched it up before it fell. "Quick hands," he said. The crystal vase, McGuffin noticed, had a brief message etched in glass: TO ISAAC STEIN, DIRECTOR, FIELDS OF FLESH, FROM BENJAMIN VOLPER, PRODUCER.

"Would you mind sitting against the wall?" Stein asked, pointing to one of the director's chairs.

"Not at all," McGuffin said, springing across the room like an obedient actor.

"Never could stand backlighting," the director mumbled, as he threw his feet up on the desk and laced his hands behind his head. "Go ahead, I'm listening," he said, closing his eyes.

McGuffin cleared his throat. Where to begin? He felt like an author trying to sell a script: I've got this great idea, CB— about a producer who commits suicide. Only we don't know if it's really suicide, or a publicity stunt, or mur- der...Instead McGuffin asked the director all the same questions about Ben Volper's disappearance that he had asked the other members of the Bronx Social Club and again received all the same answers.

"None of us saw Ben on the day he—disappeared. He was out walking on the beach when we arrived at the house."

"Did you arrive together or separately?" McGuffin asked.

"Separately. Everyone in Los Angeles drives his own car—I think it's a law," he replied lazily.

"In what order did you arrive?"

Stein shook his head impatiently. "I have no idea. Why do you ask?" McGuffin didn't answer. "You think somebody might have got there early and typed Ben's suicide mes- sage?" he asked, with an amused smile.

"It's possible," McGuffin said.

He shrugged easily and reached for a cigarette. "Ben

might have been murdered—I wouldn't rule that out. But friends don't murder friends—at least not without some reason. Cigarette?"

McGuffin shook his head. "I don't smoke."

"Rather atypical of your profession, isn't it?"

"Only as interpreted by yours," McGuffin answered.

Stein laughed. "You're okay."

"That's what David Hochman said," McGuffin remembered. "If this keeps up I might get in the Bronx Social Club."

"Not unless you were born on Tremont Avenue," Stein answered, playing with his cigarette, but not lighting it.

"You said you wouldn't be surprised if Volper was murdered?"

"I said I wouldn't rule it out," the director corrected.

"Do you have anybody in mind?"

"Yeah, but I'd just as soon not mention his name."

"Give me a hint."

Isaac Stein stared thoughtfully at his unlit cigarette for a moment, then at McGuffin. "Ben needed money for his films, a lot of money, but the banks were closed to him. Ben did quality films, the studios want blockbusters. So Ben had to look elsewhere for his money."

"Aba Ben Mahoud?"

Stein nodded. "But you didn't hear it here."

"What would Mahoud gain by killing his debtor?" McGuffin asked.

"Vengeance," Stein answered. "After all, it was good enough for Hamlet, wasn't it?"

"It's possible," McGuffin allowed. "But if Mahoud did kill Volper, he would have to have had somebody on the inside to place the suicide note in Volper's typewriter. And you and the rest of the Bronx Social Club were the only ones in the house that day."

"As far as we know," the director pointed out.

"Who found the note?"

"Jenny. She walked out of the study without saying a word—white as the sheet of paper in her hands."

"Then what happened?"

"We all read it—we thought it was a joke—we couldn't believe that he'd really—"

"You all handled the paper?"

"At a time like that, you don't think about fingerprints," he answered, sticking the cigarette in the corner of his mouth.

Somebody might have been thinking very much about fingerprints, McGuffin knew. Especially the typist, if the typist had not been Ben Volper. Once the page had been pawed by five people, it was unlikely that there would be a single legible print left.

"Didn't that seem strange?" McGuffin asked.

"What do you mean?" Stein replied.

"Think of it as a director. Your heroine unexpectedly finds her husband's suicide note in the typewriter. Does she remove it and bring it to her friends? Or does she stare at it, horrified, before crying out something that brings her friends running?"

"A good actress could do it either way," the director answered.

No help there. "How would you characterize the Volper marriage?" McGuffin asked.

"They adored each other," Stein answered.

"Jenny Lang never had any lovers?"

"None that I'm aware of."

"Okay, let's rule out murder and suicide for the moment," McGuffin said. "Is there any chance that Ben Volper is faking it just to get publicity for his new picture?"

The unlit cigarette waggled in Stein's mouth when he shook his head. "I don't think so."

"Then what do you think happened?" McGuffin asked.

Stein removed the cigarette from his mouth and dropped it on the desk. "I think he committed suicide. I didn't think so at first, but I do now. I just missed the signs."

"What signs?" McGuffin asked, leaning forward in the director's chair. It creaked and swayed and felt insecure.

"Gallows humor," Stein answered. "I think he knew that he had made his last film in Hollywood. He was being replaced by the film-school kids who know nothing about life but movies and television. Hell, we all are," he said, throwing one hand in the air. "Some of us can roll with it, others can't. Ben was supposed to be a tough guy, a producer, when in fact he was the most sensitive man I've ever known. He couldn't take what was happening, but he wasn't going to complain about it, either; God, he couldn't even sign his own suicide note. These sonsabitches! You don't know what pricks they are," he muttered.

"You sound as if you've been treated rather badly by them yourself," McGuffin observed.

"Badly?" he exclaimed, lunging suddenly out of his chair. "*Fields of Flesh* is a fucking masterpiece! And I directed it!" he said, slapping his palm loudly against his Yankee letters. "After that I submitted project after project after project to these sonsabitches and they turned down every fucking one of them! I give them a beautiful sensitive script, not expensive, and whata they give me? *Stakeout in fucking Watts!* And you know why?"

McGuffin shook his head. "Why?"

"Infantilism," he said, leaning far out over the desk, resting on two hands. With his hawk nose and hunched shoulders, he resembled a bird of prey, ready to attack. "What you got out here is nothin' but kids, twenty-nine-year-old studio heads, making movies for kids. Then when somebody like me wants to make a serious film, we're told there's no audience. It's a fucking self-fulfilling prophecy!" he shouted. "How can there be an audience if there's no product?"

"It's a problem," McGuffin admitted, his chair squeaking when he squirmed. Obviously Isaac Stein was no happier with his lot than David Hochman was with his.

Still, McGuffin wasn't yet ready to believe that the crassness of Hollywood could drive a man to suicide. At least not until he'd had a chance to talk to Aba Ben Mahoud.

He thanked Isaac Stein and apologized again for interrupting his shoot and destroying his camera.

"There are a lot more cameras where that one came from," the director assured him, walking McGuffin as far as the next office. "And even more shitty scripts."

"I hope they'll let you do a good one one of these days," McGuffin said.

Stein's secretary looked up from *Rolling Stone* and rolled her eyes wearily for McGuffin. She had heard the director's lament many times before.

"And I hope you find Ben," Stein offered, as he walked through the door with McGuffin.

The possibility of either was beginning to seem equally remote, McGuffin thought, as he walked to the exterior stairs at the end of the catwalk. Isaac Stein stood alone on the catwalk outside his office, watching as McGuffin made his way between the large empty buildings of the MGM lot. For all the gaiety and fantasy that Hollywood had produced, it now seemed a very lonely place.

6

Finding the cop in charge of the Volper case proved to be scarcely less difficult than finding Ben Volper. Missing Persons sent McGuffin to Homicide and Homicide insisted he go back to Missing Persons.

"I'm not going anywhere until you produce the detective who's in charge of the Benjamin Volper investigation." McGuffin insisted.

"Suit yourself," the desk sergeant said, reaching languidly for the phone. "You can wait there," he said, pointing to a wooden bench next to the wall.

McGuffin waited, out of earshot, while the sergeant phoned. He stared at McGuffin as he spoke, which made McGuffin think he was being described to someone at the other end. He hung up the phone and said nothing to McGuffin. Ten minutes later the phone rang, and again the sergeant studied McGuffin as he spoke. Again he hung up and said nothing.

Half an hour later the shift changed. Cops came and went, talking of football, while McGuffin waited, patient as an Eastern mystic, on the hard bench. When nearly an hour had passed, an enormous brown-skinned detective entered, spoke to the desk sergeant, then turned and glowered at McGuffin. Ambling across the room, tucking his shirt and rolls of fat under his belt, he looked to McGuffin like a sumo wrestler who had been outfitted by the worst tailor in Hong Kong.

"Amos McGuffin, the famous San Francisco private eye?"

he asked, in a voice surprisingly high for so large a man.

"Who says I'm famous?" McGuffin asked, climbing to his feet.

"Frangiapani."

McGuffin knew him, a street-smart undercover cop who had engineered one of the biggest narcotics busts in San Francisco history a few years back.

"He's a good man," McGuffin said.

"He says you're a pest and you drink too much," the fat detective added.

"Not when I'm being a pest," McGuffin corrected, sizing the detective up. He was a full head taller than McGuffin and a foot wider.

"Chan," the cop said, extending a beefy hand.

"Charlie?" McGuffin asked, watching his hand disappear in Chan's big brown mitt.

"Pedro," he said, with practiced patience. "I'm Mexican-Chinese, I'm six-six, and I weigh 260. Now *I'll* ask the questions. Come with me."

McGuffin followed him out the door and down the hall. He moved quickly for a big man, his loose clothes flapping like flags. Doors opened and closed. Police and civilians moved up and down the hall, disappearing into offices and elevators like rats in a maze. From somewhere in the building came the sound of a heavy steel door closing and a loud voice that pierced the hum of the air conditioners. If Gertrude Stein was wrong, if there really was a there to Los Angeles, the Hall of Justice may very well be it, McGuffin thought.

"Who you working for?" Chan asked, with a quick backward glance.

"Volper's father."

"Volper's got a father?" he muttered, opening the door for McGuffin. "I thought a bird shit on a fence post and hatched him."

It was the first bad word he had heard about Ben Volper. He wondered what Chan had on him.

"Sit anywhere," the detective said, closing the door with a hard slam.

The room was bare except for a folding table, several chairs, and a few ashtrays that hadn't been emptied for a long time. Even with the door closed, the vague, ambient sounds of the building continued to press, muffled, through the cracks and pores of the concrete and glass.

"Some office," McGuffin said, sliding a chair out from under the table. "Where's the bowling trophy and the picture of the kids?"

"My office is being painted," he said, sitting, with surprising delicacy, on a folding chair. The chair disappeared and the detective looked like a giant Oriental magician, levitating.

McGuffin spun a chair around and straddled it, wrapping his arms around the back.

"Okay, McGuffin, why are you here?" Chan asked.

"I'm looking for Ben Volper."

"If you're looking for Ben Volper, you should be out talking to the sharks, not to me, because as far as I'm concerned, Volper's a suicide."

"What makes you think so?" McGuffin asked.

"The clothes on the beach? The suicide note? I may not be a famous San Francisco private eye, but that's good enough for me."

"An unsigned suicide note," McGuffin added. Chan shrugged indifferently. "Did you find Volper's fingerprints on the note?"

"We found dozens of prints, all of them smeared. We presume Volper's were in there someplace too."

"Can I examine the note?" McGuffin asked, already knowing the answer. "Real" detectives did not like to be second-guessed by the "privates."

The chair groaned when the cop squirmed. "Don't be a pest, huh, McGuffin?" he pleaded. "I'm an overworked cop, the issue of two oppressed minorities. If I get a chance to close a file, I'm gonna close it. Now if you wanna keep your file open, just to keep the money coming in, that's your business. But I don't want you stirring things up with the press, or down at City Hall, or with the movie people. Because if you do, I'm gonna have to come down hard on you.

You understand?" he asked, squinting at McGuffin as if in pain.

McGuffin understood. There were "active" cops, those who liked to make arrests; and there were the "make-no-waves" sort, who were just waiting for their pension to come around. Pedro Chan obviously belonged to the latter category.

"I understand perfectly," McGuffin said.

"I sincerely hope so," Detective Chan said, getting to his feet. "Now if you've got no more questions, I'm late for my coffee break."

McGuffin had a lot of questions, but it was plain he wasn't going to get any answers from Pedro Chan. He got to his feet and allowed Chan to steer him out the door.

Walking down the hall, Chan laid a heavy hand on McGuffin's shoulder. "By the way, how is Frangiapani managing to stay alive after a big drug bust like that?"

"The usual," McGuffin shrugged, or half shrugged. The shoulder under Chan's paw wouldn't move. "He keeps a retired police dog in his apartment and wears a bulletproof vest even in the precinct house. He seems to think that if anybody gets him, it'll be another cop."

Chan shook his head. "That's no way to live." Heroics were not Chan's thing.

"Listen, Pedro, I'd like to ask a favor of you," McGuffin said.

"Sure, Amos," Pedro Chan replied with a painful squeeze.

"If you get a lead on Volper's whereabouts, would you let me know, just for his father's sake?"

His short laugh resembled a snort. "You don't really think Volper's alive, do you, McGuffin?"

"Probably not," McGuffin allowed. "But that doesn't mean he committed suicide, either."

Chan released his shoulder and stopped walking. "You think he was murdered?" he asked, wide-eyed.

McGuffin walked a few steps farther, then turned, smiling. In a town full of actors, Pedro Chan was the worst.

"If he wasn't, why is a Homicide detective handling a Missing Persons case?" McGuffin asked.

Chan hooked his thumbs in his belt and nodded slowly. "Frangiapani said you'd be a pest."

"Why don't you level with me?" McGuffin pleaded. "We're both on the same side."

"We aren't even playing the same game," Chan said. Then he turned and walked back up the hall, sweeping the floor with the cuffs of his pants.

"What about Aba Ben Mahoud?" McGuffin called.

Chan stopped, turned, and walked slowly back to where McGuffin stood. "What do you know about Aba Ben Mahoud?" he asked.

"You show me yours and I'll show you mine," McGuffin countered.

Chan studied him closely for a moment, then decided: "You're bluffing."

"You'll never know if you don't call me," McGuffin answered.

"Stay away from Mahoud," Chan ordered, sticking a fat brown finger in McGuffin's face. "Mahoud's a respectable businessman and I'm not gonna have him harassed by a pesty San Francisco shamus."

"Respectable businessmen don't kill their business partners," McGuffin replied.

"You really think Mahoud would kill Volper just because he lost a few million dollars on his pictures?" Chan asked, as if speaking to a child.

"Men have been killed for a hell of a lot less."

"But not by Mahoud!" When Chan shouted, his voice rose even higher. "Mahoud loses that much at Santa Anita in an afternoon! He's in oil, he's worth billions, you klutz! And I'm warning you, McGuffin, you go near him and I'm gonna chew your face off!" he threatened, waving a fist as big as McGuffin's head. He walked away, then turned back for one final warning. "I'm not bluffing!"

McGuffin knew he wasn't. Pedro Chan was not a man to be defied. It wasn't his size, it was his eyes. He could shoot Jackie Cooper's dog without blinking them.

McGuffin stepped out into the sunlight, leaving the hum of the Hall of Justice behind, and walked quickly to his car.

A short while later he was back in Beverly Hills, driving past manicured lawns and big Spanish houses with birds chirping in the fountains. With the sounds of the Hall of Justice still ringing in his ears, McGuffin thought it had the look of a movie set, about to be struck to make way for a new show.

7

Bel Air (so-called because of its clean air) is a mansion-covered hill rising above Beverly Hills (so-called because it's flat). To those in "the industry" (as well as to sundry civilian millionaires), it is the Olympus of the gods, the city celestial at the end of the guiding light. The architectural style is what one would expect of film stars, heterogeneous and fanciful, ranging from quaint but sensible reproductions of Versailles or the Taj Mahal to the modest English country cottages modeled on Buckingham Palace. Messengers are stationed at the foot of Olympus, dispensing sacred scrolls that purport to connect each of the many gods and goddesses with his or her kingdom.

McGuffin stopped on Sunset Boulevard to purchase one of these scrolls from a stout middle-aged messenger with bleached-blue hair, who was selling them from a shopping cart. Were this not such a usual sight, McGuffin thought, as the blowsy woman approached, waving her maps, he might be mistaken for a john about to do business with a two-dollar hooker.

"Map to the homes of the stars?" she asked, sticking her head through the window. "I got 'em all—Burt, Lori, Barbra, Jackie, Dolly...I can even tell you who's home and who's away on location."

"How much?" McGuffin asked.

"Only three-fifty and guaranteed current," she answered, thrusting one on the detective.

McGuffin gave her a five-dollar bill and told her to keep the change.

"Well, aren't you the sport?" she said, thrusting the bill into her ample bosom.

"I take it you know most of the people in Bel Air," McGuffin said, pointing up the hill.

"If I don't know 'em, they don't live there," she boasted.

"Can you tell me how to get to Aba Ben Mahoud's house?"

"Who?" she asked.

McGuffin sighed and picked up the map. "I don't suppose it would do any good to ask for my money back."

"It'd be like spittin' in the wind," she answered.

"That's what I thought," McGuffin said, reaching across the seat to roll up the window.

"But you can ask down here at the gate." She pointed.

"They'll give out that information?" he asked.

"How do you think I make these maps?" she answered.

"Thanks," McGuffin said.

He rolled up the window, then pulled confidently into the rapid stream of traffic, unmindful of honking horns and squealing tires. Only a few hundred yards farther, he pulled abruptly off the boulevard and parked beside the guard shack just inside the tall white gateposts that flanked the entrance. He got out of the car and sauntered into the gate-house with authority. A uniformed guard, sitting at the switchboard behind the counter, got to his feet when McGuffin entered.

"Don't get up," McGuffin said. "I'm just on my way up to see Aba Ben Mahoud—he said you'd give me directions."

"Who shall I say is calling?" the guard asked, turning back to the switchboard.

McGuffin's confidence remained unchanged. "No need to call, I'm expected. If you'll just give me the address..."

"Sorry," the guard said. "I have my orders."

His confidence ebbed. Oh, well, why not give it a try, he decided. "Amos McGuffin. Tell him it's about Ben Volper."

The guard relayed the message to someone at the house,

then waited for a reply. McGuffin was ready to leave, when the guard hung up and turned to him.

"Mr. Mahoud says to come right up," the guard said, scribbling the address on a slip of paper.

"He did?" McGuffin said.

"Straight up here," he said, pointing. "Bear right after the golf course, all the way to the top."

"Thanks," McGuffin said, taking the paper. "Thanks a lot."

He stumbled out of the shack and hurried to his car before Mahoud might discover his mistake. Either that, or Volper's name is the open sesame and I'm Ali Baba, McGuffin thought, as he drove up the hill.

He bore right past the lush green fairways of the Bel Air Country Club and up a steep, winding road, bordered by tall eucalyptus trees. Here and there he caught a glimpse, through gates or trees, of the incredible houses of Bel Air. One, a French chateau at the end of a long poplar-lined drive, seemed to be a cinematic illusion—McGuffin was sure there couldn't be that much level space on this mountain.

Coming out of the eucalyptus, he passed a burned hillside and the remains of a once palatial house, reduced now to foundation and dirt-filled swimming pool. At least God's not intimidated by these people, McGuffin thought.

Aba Ben Mahoud's house was on the last ridge, just below the peak of the hill. A tall iron gate opened, as if by magic, when McGuffin turned in the drive. Is it the magic of electronics, or am I being watched? McGuffin wondered, as the gates fell shut with a solid clank.

The house lay at the bottom of a gently sloping, U-shaped drive, a mosquelike pink building perched giddily on the edge of a steep ravine. He parked in front of the door, got out, and rang the bell. Almost immediately, the door was opened by a large Arab who hadn't shaved for a few days. He wore a rumpled black suit over a dirty white shirt, but no tie. Mahoud's "spring," McGuffin knew, even before he spied the telltale shoulder holster peeking out from under his jacket. McGuffin was a keen student of bodyguards, or springs, as he called them. In his business he often came up against them. Some were large but lacked the killer instinct—ex-college footballers just waiting for something better to come along—while others, the samurai class, would willingly kill or be killed at the slightest signal from their master. This latter class could be identified by a keen student of the profession, which McGuffin was, by the look of criminal insanity that burned in the eye. This Arab, McGuffin decided, had it in spades. The Arab watched closely as McGuffin reached slowly and carefully for his business card. The spring took it with little interest.

"Amos McGuffin?" he explained, thinking perhaps the Arab couldn't read English. "I called a few minutes ago?" McGuffin was beginning to think the man might be deaf and dumb, until he stepped aside and allowed McGuffin to enter, then softly closed the door.

In the center of the entry hall was a large fountain filled with minutely detailed statues of naked women pouring water over one another. McGuffin started toward the fountain, but was stopped by a clamp on the shoulder.

"Just wanted to say hello to the girls," McGuffin mumbled, as the spring's hands went professionally over his body. "Keep it clean," he said, as hands ran up his legs. He could afford to be relaxed, he had left his gun at the hotel. Or could he? he wondered, when the spring had finished.

The spring signaled McGuffin to follow him across the mosaic tile foyer. He had taps on his pointy black shoes, which clacked monotonously the length of the corridor. At the end of the hall, the spring opened a heavy door to a book-lined library.

"And I thought Angelenos didn't read," McGuffin said to no one, as he surveyed the walls. The books were expensive but looked unread, in their lustrous red leather, gleaming in the light that passed through the enormous stained-glass window. The tables in the large room—there were several—were strewn with newspapers and periodicals, some in Arabic, but most in French, German, or English. *Someone* is doing some reading, McGuffin observed,

as he leafed through a French magazine. An article on Iran—
it was the only word he recognized in the French title—
was heavily underlined and annotated.

"Do you read French?" a voice from the doorway inquired.

Letting the magazine fall to the table, McGuffin looked
up at Aba Ben Mahoud. Hard as thong leather, was Mc-
Guffin's first thought. Just under six feet, he was lean and
taut, with deep facial lines and wavy, almost kinky, salt-
and-pepper hair, cut close at the sides.

"Scarcely," McGuffin answered.

"Pity," he said. "I am Aba Ben Mahoud."

"Amos McGuffin."

"I am pleased to make your acquaintance," he said, in
only slightly accented English, as he shook McGuffin's hand.
"I must apologize for the—frisk?" McGuffin nodded. "My
life has been threatened," he said, with a gesture implying
that it happened all the time.

"By who?" McGuffin asked.

"Whom? No one you know," he said. "Please, have a
seat."

They each sat in one of the club chairs beside the coffee
table, which was piled high with more periodicals.

"Someone does a lot of reading," McGuffin observed.

"It is my one pleasure in life. Can I get you something
to drink?" he asked, glancing over his shoulder at the spring,
who stood ready at the doorway.

McGuffin declined and Mahoud signaled the spring out
of the room with a wave of one finger. They don't bite their
masters, McGuffin said to himself, as he watched the spring
disappear.

"You have information about my friend Mr. Volper?" he
asked, making a tent with his hands.

"I'm gathering information about Mr. Volper," McGuffin
corrected. "His father hired me to find him." Mahoud seemed
disappointed. "I'm sorry—if you thought I was here about
the money he owes you..."

"No, no—not at all," he said quickly. "The money means
even less to me than it did to Ben. For each of us, it's just

a way of getting things done. That, I think, is the reason we were such good friends."

"Were?"

Mahoud nodded. "I'm afraid Ben did exactly what he said he was going to do."

"He told you he was going to commit suicide?"

"Not in those words, but he said as much. Ben was extremely despondent because the system would not allow him to make the films he wished to make."

"But he was making films outside the system, with your money," McGuffin reminded him.

Mahoud smiled and shook his head. "Mine was a small contribution. Ben was forced to rely on the major studios for money and distribution. He knew what would be acceptable and what would not. He couldn't continue to work under those conditions, so he killed himself," the Arab said easily. To him it was plain and simple.

But not to McGuffin. "I can't believe he'd kill himself," he said firmly. "Not just because he couldn't make the films he wanted to make."

"The history of art is replete with such sacrifice," the Arab said, with a schoolmasterly rotundity.

"They only sacrificed themselves when there was absolutely no hope," McGuffin said, with the assurance of a barroom philosopher. "Volper spent his entire career struggling against the system—successfully. There was no reason for him to quit now."

Mahoud smiled easily. "Perhaps you are right." McGuffin would get no argument from him.

"If I might ask a personal question, Mr. Mahoud. You're an Arab and Ben Volper is—or was—a Jew. How did you happen to be such close friends?"

"Ben is—or was—a progressive Jew; I am a progressive Arab," he said, folding his tent and sitting stiffly in his chair. "We both understood that the future of Israel and the stability of the entire Middle East require a unity of purpose." Again he sounded like a college professor.

"Unity of purpose—" McGuffin repeated, like a dull student.

"Exactly," he said, with a quick, single nod. He was not going to waste his time explaining complicated political theory to a private eye.

"May I ask what business you're in?"

"Oil," Mahoud answered. That was all.

"And movies?" McGuffin prodded.

"I invest in artists whose work I value. I don't consider that business," he answered.

"Must be nice," McGuffin observed, looking about the luxurious library.

"I'm sorry I can't be of more help," Mahoud said, sliding forward on the smooth leather chair. The interview was coming to a close.

"Did you invest in Volper's last picture?" McGuffin asked quickly.

"A small sum," Mahoud said dismissively.

"How small?"

"A million, perhaps."

"Do you expect to get it back?"

"I have no idea. I must ask Victor," he reminded himself.

"Victor?"

"Victor Wenner, the director of *Lemmings*," he explained. "He is Ben's protégé. If there is nothing else, Mr. McGuffin," he said, climbing out of the leather chair, "I'm sorry that I don't have more time."

"That's all right," McGuffin said, following him to his feet. At the door, McGuffin stopped and turned for a last look at the library. "At least on this job I'm getting to see some beautiful houses."

Mahoud smiled. He accompanied McGuffin as far as the hall, where the spring waited to show him to the door, wordlessly.

"Nice talking to you," McGuffin said, as the spring closed the door on him.

He got into his car and drove back down the hill to Sunset and on to the Beverly Hills Hotel. It was a short drive and he was back in his room in only a few minutes. He walked directly to the phone and asked the operator to put him through to the Screen Directors Guild.

"I'd like Victor Wenner's phone number," he informed the woman at the Guild office.

"May I know your name and the nature of your business?" she asked.

"My name is McGuffin. I'm Ben Volper's legal representative. I have some money for Mr. Wenner for directorial services on Mr. Volper's last film, *Lemmings*."

"You can send it to the Guild; we'll see that he gets it," she said.

"Fine, I'll do that," McGuffin promised. "But I have to talk to Mr. Wenner first, just to clarify a few things."

Finally, reluctantly, McGuffin was given the number.

"Thanks," McGuffin said, scribbling the phone number on hotel stationery. "By the way, if I were a producer and I wanted to hire one of your members, would you give me his number?" he asked.

"I'm afraid we couldn't give out that information," she answered.

"Keep up the good work," McGuffin said, as he dropped the receiver in its cradle.

He dialed the number he had been given and again the phone was answered by a woman, this one pleasant-voiced.

"I'm sorry, Vic's not here right now. This is Erin, can I help?"

McGuffin identified himself and told her he'd like to talk to Victor about his boss's disappearance.

"Thank God, Vic should talk to somebody," she said, speaking quickly and breathlessly.

"Why is that?" McGuffin asked.

"Because he won't talk to me and I know something's bothering him," she answered. "You want to come by tonight? He'll be back around eight."

"Eight'll be fine," McGuffin said.

She gave him the address. "That's off Hollywood Boulevard, before you get to Vine," she added.

"I'll find it."

"Around eight," she repeated.

She seemed anxious that he be there.

8

The address was that of a rococo palace of the twenties, with onion towers and peacock-feather escutcheons, the perfect symbol of the good old days in Hollywood, when architects, like movie makers, were free to indulge their wildest fantasies. Once grand, it was now collapsing, piece by piece, like the sign above the Hollywood Hills. Slabs of stucco had fallen away, revealing rotted lath. Some windows were boarded up, others merely broken, and large sections of Mexican tile were missing from the lobby walls. Those mailboxes that weren't broken bore the pathetic names of hopeless film or recording businesses, most of them ending grandiosely with "Enterprises."

McGuffin found Wenner's bell. It was labeled VICTOR WENNER, DIRECTOR and, below that, ERIN GREEN, FILM EDITOR. He pushed the button and waited. There was no answer, but after a few minutes, the lobby door was opened by a harried young woman in jeans and an oversized sweatshirt.

"Mr. McGuffin?" she asked quickly. She wore a pile of pumpkin-colored hair, loosely fastened atop her head to reveal a long, slender neck. She had the lean, hard body of an athlete and the square-jawed, high-cheekbone look of the tomboy model.

"That's me." He smiled. He liked her immediately.

"Erin," she said, shaking his hand and pulling him inside, all in one motion. "I gotta get back, I left the spaghetti sauce on." She released him and skipped across the lobby to the stairs.

"Go ahead, I'll follow," McGuffin said, admiring her long legs and taut little ass as she leaped at the stairs, gobbling them up two by two.

"Fourth floor!" she called, already rounding the first flight.

"Jesus," McGuffin muttered, after the third flight. Accustomed as he was to the hills of San Francisco, these stairs were tiring him out.

"Keep coming!" she called from the floor above.

The green door at the end of the short hall was open. He stepped into a faintly lit room, crammed with tables covered with film-editing equipment. Strings, from which snippets of film hung, were stretched across the room like clotheslines. A faint light shined through from the back of the loft, like a campfire in a cellophane forest.

"Back here!" she called.

The cellophane rustled like dry bones when he pushed through to the back of the room. She stood over a steaming pot, stirring spaghetti sauce with a long wooden spoon. It smelled good.

"Vic should be here in a little while. You must be early," she said, dividing her attention between him and the sauce.

"It's after eight-thirty," McGuffin pointed out.

"Is it? He said he'd be here at seven, but I always allow an hour. I guess I'll have to start allowing more. Would you like a glass of wine while you wait?" she asked, quickly brushing the hair from her forehead with the back of her hand.

There was an open half gallon of cheap red wine and a filled glass on the sink counter. McGuffin desperately wanted a drink—he had been dry for more than seventy-two hours and it was getting worse instead of better—but he shook his head and turned away. The next twenty-four hours would be the litmus test, he knew from past experience. "Not while I'm working," he said.

"Okay," she said, reaching for her glass.

Rather than watch her drink, McGuffin walked across the

kitchen and peeked behind the Indian curtains in the alcove. There was a mattress on the floor and a television set with a bent coat hanger for an aerial.

"Interesting place," he said.

"It's a pigsty," she said. "We're just waiting for some money so we can split."

McGuffin was surprised. "Didn't your husband make some money for directing *Lemmings?*" he asked.

"He deferred almost everything," she said. "And so did I for editing. Love and deferments, that's the way Ben made all his pictures. By the way, we're not married, just living together," she added, as she tasted her sauce. She smacked her lips and pushed the wooden spoon at McGuffin. "Tell me if it needs more salt."

McGuffin walked across the kitchen and sampled the spaghetti sauce. "Tastes all right to me."

"Maybe a little," she said, reaching for the salt carton. "Vic likes a lot of salt." She poured some in her hand and scattered it over the sauce, then brushed off her hands and reached for her glass of wine. "I could get smashed waiting for that guy."

He wanted to ask why she waited, but he didn't. Instead, he asked: "Why would you and Vic work for Volper without pay?" When she drank, McGuffin swallowed with her.

"Because he's the only guy in this town who has any integrity," she answered. "And warm? My God, like a Jewish mother!" she exclaimed suddenly. "Vic and I met him while we were in New York, and he said if we ever get out to L.A. we should give him a call—you know, that kind of bullshit. Only with him it wasn't bullshit. He introduced us to a lot of people, he got us work....We owe him a lot," she said.

"A generous man," McGuffin commented.

"The best."

"Scarcely a potential suicide victim," McGuffin observed.

"Yeah, how do you figure that?" she asked.

"I don't know. His friends all seem to think he was suicidal. Was he two different people?"

"Vic seems to think so. I never saw it."

"Vic thinks he killed himself?"

She removed the spoon from the spaghetti sauce and tossed it into the sink. Then she ran cold water over the spoon and watched the spaghetti sauce trickle down the drain. "I don't know what Vic is thinking," she answered, shutting off the water. "We had big plans before this. We were going to follow *Lemmings* to the festivals, we were going to parlay it into another film—we were even thinking about getting married. And now he's put everything on hold."

"Because of what happened to Volper?"

"I don't know why," she answered. She took a sip of wine, then clanked her glass heavily on the drainboard. She gripped the edge of the sink and stared at the drain. McGuffin watched her shoulders droop as she sighed silently.

"What's wrong, Erin?" McGuffin asked.

"Everything," she blurted, and groped for the dish towel on the sink counter. McGuffin waited while she dried her eyes. Finished, she turned to him and smiled quickly. "Sorry." Her eyes were very green and her cheeks were flushed, as if they had been dusted lightly with paprika. She looked soft and damp and vulnerable. And quite beautiful.

"If I knew you better, I'd take you in my arms and make you tell me all about it," McGuffin said.

"Maybe that's just what I need," she said, smiling through her tears.

When McGuffin opened his arms, she pressed against him and clutched him tightly. He could feel her breasts, small and firm, pressing against his chest.

"Does Vic know anything about Ben Volper's disappearance?" he asked.

"I don't think it has anything to do with Ben," she said. "Vic was shocked; so was I. But it's something else."

"What?" McGuffin prodded, gliding his hand lightly across her back. She wore no bra.

"I don't know. Maybe it's the drugs." She sighed, coming out of McGuffin's arms. She dried her eyes on the sleeve of her sweatshirt and smiled fleetingly again.

"Vic is into drugs?" McGuffin asked.

"Just coke—no big deal," she said. "Everybody out here does it—Hollywood beer—I do it myself. It never got to him before, but maybe it finally has. They say it does, you know—fries your brain." She ran her hand through her hair and walked across the floor to no particular place. "I don't know—I just know he's going through some changes and he won't open up to me and it's making me crazy!"

On this, they both heard Vic thrashing through the cellophane. When he saw McGuffin, he froze, not with surprise, but with fear, it seemed to McGuffin.

"Vic!" she exclaimed, and hurried across the room to kiss him. He continued to stare warily at McGuffin as she kissed him lightly on the lips. "Where've you been? We've been waiting," she admonished lightly.

"Who's he?" the young director demanded. He was thin, almost emaciated, with sallow skin and straight black hair. He needed a shave, and his clothes looked as if they had been slept in for the past few nights.

"Amos McGuffin; I'm a detective. Ben Volper's father hired me to find him," McGuffin said, advancing with outstretched hand.

Wenner looked away, glared angrily at Erin, then lunged past her, through the Indian curtains and into the tiny bedroom.

"Victor?" she said. She looked helplessly at McGuffin, then followed Victor into the alcove.

"I'm not talking to any detective!" Wenner shouted.

Erin tried to hush him. "He's only trying to help," she pleaded.

"I don't want any help!" he shouted at her.

McGuffin walked across the kitchen to the alcove and pulled the curtain back. Wenner stood beside the bed, facing the wall, as if he were urinating, while his girl friend stood beside him.

"Why should *you* need help?" McGuffin asked.

He glanced over his shoulder at the detective, then back at the wall. "I don't have to talk to you." he said.

"No, you don't *have* to talk to me," McGuffin agreed. "But it might do you some good if you did."

"Just get out of here and leave me alone!" Wenner ordered.

"Victor, please—talk to him," Erin urged. "Tell him what's wrong. I'll go downstairs if you like. I won't listen."

"Goddamnit there's nothing wrong to talk about. I keep telling you that. Whose side are you on anyway?" He glared and fairly spat the words at her.

"She's on your side, kid, so stop hollering at her," McGuffin ordered. He could take only so much childish hysteria, then he spanked.

"This is my apartment, I'll holler if I want!" he shouted, louder than ever, as he turned and pointed to the door. "And you can get out! Just get the fuck out of here before I call the police!"

"Shit," McGuffin muttered as he took a step forward, open hand raised.

"No!" Erin shouted and jumped at McGuffin.

McGuffin allowed her to pull his hand down and push him out of the room. He was glad she was there. Private investigators' licenses are lifted for a lot less than slapping recalcitrant witnesses.

"I'm sorry," McGuffin apologized. "He's getting hysterical…"

"I know, just leave him alone and let me talk to him," she said, pushing him to the door.

"Is he on something?"

"A little coke, that's all," she said. "You can talk to him when he comes down. he'll be all right then."

The two of them spilled out into the hall, and she pulled the door partly closed. McGuffin removed a card from his pocket and handed it to her.

"Get him to talk to me," he said. "It's very important; I'm sure he knows something."

"Yes, yes," she agreed, nodding quickly, anxious to have him gone.

"Will you be all right?"

"Yes, I'll be fine. Oh, shit, I wish I had a Valium!" she wailed.

"Call me at the Beverly Hills Hotel," McGuffin ordered.

"Call me at the Beverly Hills Hotel," McGuffin ordered.

"I will," she said, trying to close the door on him.

"Promise?"

"Promise," she said.

He wondered if she would. One way or another, Mc-Guffin had to talk to that kid. He knew something and it was eating him up.

9

McGuffin was awakened from a sound sleep by the ringing of the phone. Eyes closed, he moved his hand crablike over the nightstand until he found the offending instrument.

"Hello."

"Mr. McGuffin?" A woman's voice.

"Yes." He opened his eyes. Unfamiliar as he was with this time of the day, he remembered what sunrise looked like. "Jesus—what time is it?"

"I waited as long as I could. Vic hasn't come home!"

"Erin?" McGuffin said, pushing himself up in bed.

"He went out last night after you left and he hasn't come home yet! I'm afraid something may have happened to him and I don't know who to call or what to do, so I called you. You said I could."

"Yeah, that's fine. Just take it easy and tell me what happened," he said soothingly.

"Well, there was a phone call after you left," she began, trying to be calm. "I don't know who it was, he wouldn't tell me. He just hung up the phone and said he had to go out and then he went."

"Did he say where he was going?"

"He wouldn't tell me."

"Was the call from a man or a woman?" McGuffin asked.

"I told you, I don't know," she answered impatiently.

"All right, don't get excited," McGuffin said quickly. "If I'm going to help you, I have to know a few things."

"Like what?"

74

"Like does Vic have a girl friend?"

"No," she replied firmly.

"Are you sure?"

"Positive. When he's doing coke, he's not interested in sex."

"Maybe he went out to get some more?" McGuffin suggested.

"Sex?"

"Cocaine. Maybe that was his connection on the phone."

"Shit, we've got bags of the stuff all over the place," she said. "Why would he go out for it?"

"I thought you said he was a light user."

"So I lied."

"What else did you lie about?"

"Nothing. Oh shit, I never should have called you. First Ben disappears and now Vic, and all you want to know about is drugs. I'm sorry I bothered you."

"Don't hang up," McGuffin ordered.

"God, I don't know what to do," she said, with a tremor in her voice.

"Don't cry—please, it won't do any good," he begged. And besides, he hated to hear a woman cry, especially so early in the morning. "He's probably out buzzing the neighborhood. When the coke wears off, he'll come back down."

"I don't think so," she said, with a grave certainty that gave McGuffin pause.

"Okay, you stay there, I'll call the police," he said.

"Thank you, Mr. McGuffin," she said, with a sigh of relief.

"And stop calling me Mr. McGuffin, it makes me feel old," he told her.

"Yes, sir," she said.

McGuffin hung up, then rang the desk and asked to be put through to Hollywood police headquarters. An uninterested woman cop was finally persuaded to take Mc-Guffin's call.

"Is this an emergency?" she interrupted, as McGuffin began his report.

"It could be," McGuffin answered.

When he had given her the information, and after she

had promised to send "the first available car" to the Wenner apartment, McGuffin rolled over and went back to sleep for a few more hours. He wasn't particularly worried. Victor Wenner, he had decided the night before, was an asshole. And assholes have a way of showing up wherever you go.

When he next awoke it was a little after nine, a reasonable hour for a reasonably ambitious private detective to rise. He showered and shaved and, with considerable trepidation, climbed back into his Robert Kirk tweeds. Today was the day, he promised himself, he would get a new suit—one of those cotton cord jobs that would come in handy in San Francisco for one or two days every summer.

He had a bagel and cream cheese in the coffee shop, while he leisurely read the *Times*. The President was blaming Congress for unemployment and Congress was pushing a public works bill. You have to give Los Angeles one thing, McGuffin conceded, as he turned the last page of the *Times*. Their newspaper is better than San Francisco's.

He was on his way through the lobby, en route to Brooks Brothers to buy one of those wrinkly suits, when he decided to give Erin a call. By now Victor should be back and, his bile spent, more receptive to conversation.

But Victor wasn't back.

"Were the police there?" McGuffin asked.

"The police couldn't care less," she complained. "When I told them we'd had a fight, they just folded their books and left."

"Okay, I'll see what I can do." McGuffin sighed. "Stay close to the phone."

"Thank you, Amos," she said.

At the sound of his first name, he saw her face, and his reddened as it hadn't in years. It annoyed him. He was too old to be affected this way by a beautiful young redhead.

"You're welcome," he growled.

Chan probably wouldn't care any more about the missing director than the other cops had, but he was the only L.A. police contact he had.

"Detective Chan, Homicide," McGuffin instructed the switchboard operator.

"We got a Chan, but not in Homicide," she answered.

"Pedro Chan?" McGuffin asked, as he was abruptly cut off by the ringing phone. On the second ring, the phone was picked up.

"Narcotics, Chan speaking," a familiar high voice replied.

"Narcotics?" McGuffin exclaimed.

An image of Chan's cold dark eyes flashed familiarly in McGuffin's brain. He remembered where he had seen such eyes: he had known narcs who were also junkies—it was an occupational hazard. They moved through the drug underworld almost entirely on their own, getting high and making small hits just often enough to avoid suspicion; letting the little fish go, waiting patiently to make a case against the big dealer. If he's lucky, a narc might make one good case in his career, as Frangiapani had. After that he's "made" and his days as an undercover doper are over. If he can control his habit he'll be given a desk and allowed to do some drugs on the side, discreetly, nothing to embarrass the department. And if he's incredibly lucky, the friends of the guys he put away won't find him one night when he's strung out on the shit and stick a syringe in his heart.

"McGuffin?" Chan asked after a long pause.

"What's Volper's disappearance got to do with narcotics?" McGuffin asked.

"Don't be a pest, McGuffin," he warned, his voice deepening a full octave with threat.

"It's Mahoud, isn't it?" McGuffin went on. "He's the dealer, the Middle East connection. Volper was working for Mahoud—"

"Back off," Chan warned.

"So was Victor Wenner."

"Who's Victor Wenner?"

"The guy who showed up missing last night. You know what I think, Chan?"

"Don't think, McGuffin. Get on the plane and fly back to Frisco."

"I think Volper and Wenner were selling cocaine for Mahoud, but decided to go into business for themselves and Mahoud killed them. And I think you know that too, but you won't bust him until somebody forces your hand, so I'm gonna help you out."

"Wait a minute, McGuffin!" Chan cut in, his voice high again.

"Wenner may still be alive—"

"Don't go near Mahoud! I'm ordering you!"

"If you don't want to see two more dead, you better get up to Mahoud's place right away!"

Chan's voice was shrill but garbled as McGuffin hung up on him. He hurried through the lobby and skipped down the front stairs, where a group of hotel guests waited for their cars. He moved to the head of the line and handed the attendant a twenty.

"Right now," he ordered.

The attendant took off at a run, leaving the waiting guests grumbling loudly.

"Police business," McGuffin confided.

They were dubious, but they settled down.

McGuffin drove as fast as he could without piling up, snaking up the Bel Air hillside on screeching tires. He turned into Mahoud's drive and squealed to a stop only a few inches from the locked gate. When he got out of the car and pressed the button on the fence, a curtain moved at a second-floor window. Whether it was Mahoud or his spring, he couldn't tell, but, surprisingly, the gate opened.

McGuffin parked carelessly and hurried to the front door, already opening.

"I want to see your boss," he told the spring. "Don't worry, I'm not carrying a gun," McGuffin assured him, extending his arms.

"It's all right!" Mahoud called from the top of the stairs, as the spring moved to search McGuffin. "I'm sure Mr. McGuffin means us no harm."

McGuffin waited as Mahoud walked down the stairs. He was dressed to go out, in a sharply pressed brown suit. Or perhaps he had just come in, McGuffin thought—from disposing of Victor Wenner. If he had, there was always room for one more in the grave, McGuffin knew. Hurry, Chan.

"Sorry to bother you again, Mr. Mahoud, but something's come up and I thought you ought to know about it," McGuffin called over the splashing fountain.

Mahoud stopped at the foot of the stairs, keeping the fountain between them. "Yes?"

"Victor is missing."

"Victor?" he repeated.

"Wenner," McGuffin said, pronouncing it clearly. "I understood he worked for you."

"Ah, yes, the director," Mahoud remembered.

"That's right, the director."

"But he didn't work for me, only for Ben," Mahoud corrected.

McGuffin nodded. "Of course. You only invest in causes with which you're sympathetic. Your real business is oil, isn't it?"

"That's right."

"So I don't suppose there's anything I could tell you about niblicks or confluting valves, is there?" McGuffin said, with a self-deprecating laugh.

"Hardly. Mr. McGuffin, would you mind telling me specifically why you've come?" Mahoud asked, starting across the foyer.

"I've come to talk about your real business," McGuffin answered, shifting his tone suddenly.

Mahoud stopped, still keeping the naked bathers between himself and the detective. "I've told you, Mr. McGuffin, my only business is oil."

"Come on, Mr. Mahoud...A niblick is a golf club and a confluting valve is something I just made up. If you're in the oil business, I'm a male nurse," McGuffin said, moving around the fountain toward Mahoud.

If there had been a signal from Mahoud, McGuffin hadn't seen it. He vaguely felt a dull blow to the back of the head, saw Mahoud's face recede from focus and then the bright tiles, rushing at him as if they were meteorites out of *Star Wars*.

He next became aware of someone handling him with little concern for his well-being, dragging him down stairs, and dropping him roughly onto cool cement smelling of stale dust. A bare bulb, like a clapper, swung from the ceiling throwing light and shadow across the room in a steadily diminishing pattern. Things began to form—he was in a dusty cellar, a wine cellar, lying on his back among shelves of wine, hundreds and hundreds of bottles, stretching beyond the swinging light—and the back of his head was beginning to hurt like a sonofabitch, which was a good sign. In a business where trauma was an occupational hazard, McGuffin had learned that serious concussions hurt less than minor ones.

"Get up, Mr. McGuffin," Mahoud ordered.

McGuffin sat up, rubbed the back of his head, and came away with a little blood. The spring lifted him under the arms and sat him on a wooden chair under the swinging light.

"Can you understand me?" Mahoud asked.

"Yeah, I can understand," McGuffin mumbled.

"Good. Because I'm going to ask you some questions, Mr. McGuffin. And how you answer them will have a great effect on your life. So please, answer each question fully and honestly," Mahoud urged, as the swinging bulb moved back and forth behind his head, bathing his face in dizzying shadows. When McGuffin raised one hand to block the light, Mahoud pulled it down.

"Why are you interested in my business? Who are you working for?" he demanded.

"The police know I'm here," McGuffin muttered, his words slurred.

"You're a poor liar, Mr. McGuffin."

"You'll see," McGuffin said. Hurry, Chan.

"And a very reckless man." The swinging bulb came slowly to a halt behind Mahoud's head, framing him in a halo of white light. Strands of hair, escaped from tight waves, stood crookedly in the glow like sizzled snakes. "Other than that, I know very little about you. But before long I'll know everything there is to know about you," he said, with a nod in the direction of the spring.

Out of the corner of his eye, McGuffin saw the spring move, and he braced himself for the blow that never came. Instead, the spring took a bottle of wine from the shelf and handed it to Mahoud.

"Do you drink, Mr. McGuffin?" Mahoud asked, studying the dusty bottle.

"Not for a long time," McGuffin answered.

"I myself don't, for religious reasons, so I know nothing of wine. Château Lafite-Rothschild—is that a good one?"

"What year?" McGuffin asked.

"1964."

"Not bad," McGuffin allowed.

Mahoud smiled. He knew more about wine than his religion would allow him to admit. "Then we'll start with this one," he said, handing the bottle to the spring, who neatly smashed the neck against the edge of the wine rack, spilling little wine. He selected a silver goblet from a shelf and handed it and the wine to his boss. Mahoud filled the goblet, using almost half the bottle.

"Now we're going to play one of those drinking games American college boys are so fond of," he said, handing McGuffin the goblet. "I'm going to ask you questions and each time I get the wrong answer, you're going to drink this glass of wine—what is the word I'm looking for?" he asked.

"Chugalug?"

"Yes, chugalug."

"Sounds fair to me," McGuffin said. "Let's get started."

"Fine. The first question, then: Who are you working for?"

"Nat Volpersky."

"That's a lie."

"Chugalug?" McGuffin asked.

"Chugalug," Mahoud replied with a nod.

McGuffin raised the goblet and sniffed the wine. The bouquet was exquisite. "To your health," he toasted, and downed the '64 Lafite-Rothschild in several gulps, followed by a supremely satisfied sigh. "A bit corky," he said, extending the empty goblet to Mahoud. "But wonderful body."

"The next question," Mahoud said, as he filled the goblet a second time. "Who are you working for?"

"Nat Volpersky," McGuffin said, as he again raised the goblet.

"Get another bottle," Mahoud ordered the spring.

"How about a Saint-Émilion this time?" McGuffin suggested.

On the selfsame seventh question, the pleasure now long gone, McGuffin threw up on Mahoud's shoes. Mahoud muttered an Arabic curse and danced away, but too late.

"No more—I'm not takin' another drink," McGuffin slurred.

"Very well," Mahoud said, wiping at his shoes with a handkerchief. "Then we will have to introduce an Arabic ingredient into this American game. For every glass of wine you refuse to drink, you will lose one finger."

As he spoke, the spring opened his coat and removed an ugly hunting knife from the sheath at his belt.

"Okay," McGuffin said, extending his empty glass. "But can't we change the question?"

"Who are you working for?" Mahoud repeated for the eighth time as he filled McGuffin's glass.

On the ninth question he passed out. He awoke, face down in his own vomit, alone in the cellar. But they'd be back. Mahoud would keep pouring wine down his throat until he was satisfied he knew nothing. Then he would kill him, just as he had Ben Volper and Victor Wenner. Chan wouldn't come, he knew. That sonofabitch—goldbrick fuckin' cop! I gotta get outta here, he told himself. Just to kill Chan.

He began crawling, first on his stomach like a snake, then on his hands and knees. "Knee-walkin' drunk," he muttered. Luckily I've had some experience.

He crawled between two rows of bottles, with only a vague notion that a door lay at the end of this long corridor. He was right. He ran his fingers along the edge of the tightly closed door, found the knob, and pulled himself to his knees.

Then, bracing one hand against the doorpost, he turned and pulled. The door opened easily.

"You might make it," McGuffin whispered to himself, as he started up the stairs on hands and knees in the pitch black.

At the top of the stairs, he felt a rough wood wall, but he could find no door. He seemed to be in a long, narrow closet, scarcely three feet wide. Had he not been on his hands and knees, he might have missed the light glowing through a thin crack at the floor. When he pushed, the panel rolled out into the room and McGuffin scrabbled after it. He was in the library, empty except for himself.

He crawled to the desk and pulled himself slowly to his feet. There was little feeling in his body, but his limbs were beginning to work from memory. The thing to do now was get to the front door and out into the street before Mahoud returned, he told himself.

McGuffin lurched stiffly in the direction of the fuzzy doorway, then stopped at the faint sound of the spring's pointy tap shoes on the tile floor. It was hard to think—the way was blocked. Hide, a voice instructed. Where? He spied the couch between himself and the stained-glass window, staggered across the room, and collapsed behind it. Wait till they go downstairs, then run for it, he told himself.

When the sounds of the taps on the tile suddenly ceased, McGuffin knew they were in the library, walking across the rug. When he heard the panel close, he would bolt for the hall. Then, a moment before Mahoud shouted, McGuffin remembered...The door from the basement—he had left it open!

"The door! There he is, behind the couch!" Mahoud shouted, a split second later.

McGuffin stood, wobbly, as the spring, in no hurry, came for him. The only glimmer of freedom McGuffin could see now was the sunlight shining through the large stained-glass window in front of him. He didn't know what lay beyond that window besides sunlight. He could stay and surely die of alcoholic poisoning, or dive through the window into an unknown void.

Quickly, before he could think about it, McGuffin dived forward and crashed through the window, hurtling through the air in an explosion of brightly colored glass and dull gray lead. He kept his eyes closed tightly, for what seemed like minutes, while he waited for the crash of frail flesh and bone against the boulders and jagged rocks below. He heard and felt the snapping of limbs and brush and opened his eyes to the yellow clay that rushed up at him. The dreaded impact arrived, but he was still alive, rolling over and over through more brush, and coming finally to a stop.

He felt no broken bones or lacerations when he pulled himself half erect and plunged through the shrubbery below. He had no plan—he must keep moving and down was the only way. He heard a gunshot, followed quickly by another and the twang of a slug caroming off a rock somewhere nearby.

When he fell off a concrete retaining wall into a row of neatly trimmed hedges, he knew he had stumbled into somebody's backyard, but he couldn't see anything through the dense foliage. He crawled between the wall and the bushes, safe for the moment, he thought, until he heard voices above, shouted Arabic instructions or curses, and the sound of dirt and rocks tumbling down the hillside.

The sonsabitches! They would follow him all the way to the police station. He was becoming aware of the pain now, drumming a blunt message from deep in his body and a shrill screech from his lacerated flesh, but he pulled himself up and went on. He couldn't stop anywhere. They would follow him into a house and kill him and anyone else there. He had to lose them, get completely away from them, get to the bottom of the hill. The spring was coming, slipping and sliding, shouting and cursing, closer and closer. Don't think, run. Run and run and run.

He ran across a smooth green lawn, littered with croquet balls, then down a few steps to a swimming pool where a woman stood, clutching two small children, terrified.

"Police!" McGuffin called hoarsely, as a bullet whined off the concrete.

He was running toward a house when, for no clear reason—thoughts came like bolts of lightning in the darkness, briefly and insufficiently lighting the landscape—he suddenly veered off into the next yard. McGuffin had no way of knowing that Mahoud was in a car, patrolling the street in front of that very house at that moment. He continued to run, down a long manicured lawn, through a gate, past other houses, through a strip of trees, hoarse breath burning, blood and sweat blurring his vision, down, down—until he could run no more.

Crawling now, across an incredibly smooth cushion of grass. Mustn't stop, he kept telling himself. Crawl! Crawl, crawl, crawl! Through sand now—hot dry sand, an endless desert—crawling, crawling...

That was the last thing he remembered before he felt a gun pressing against his ribs. Or so it seemed. He lay very still, face pressed against the hot sand, and waited for the end to come.

"You, get up out of there!" an angry, imperious voice demanded.

It was not a gun poking him in the ribs, McGuffin saw, as he twisted awkwardly and painfully for a look, but a golf club. And they were not Arabs standing in the sand, but four silver-haired golfers in plaid pants and bright sweaters.

"The fellow's a mess," the one in the pink sweater muttered distastefully.

"How would a wino get in here?" the prodder with the golf club wondered aloud.

"Where am I?" McGuffin asked, struggling painfully to his hands and knees.

"The Bel Air Country Club," the prodder answered.

"Don't let the Arabs in," McGuffin pleaded.

"Not bloody likely," the gentleman in the pink sweater replied.

10

They held McGuffin prisoner in the locker room while they waited for the police, but McGuffin didn't complain. The Arabs, he knew, would be waiting patiently for his expulsion from the vaunted precincts of the Bel Air Country Club. Just this once, McGuffin found himself thankful for the caste system. He had tried, drunkenly, to explain the reason for his being in one of their sand traps, but they weren't buying it. In their perfectly ordered world, one strayed into a bunker only as the result of a mis-hit shot, not as the result of being shot at. So McGuffin waited, using the time to nurse his wounds and throw up once more, until the police, in the form of Pedro Chan, arrived.

"It's about time," McGuffin muttered, when Chan came through the door like an angry elephant.

"Can you walk?" Chan demanded.

"Yeah, I can walk," McGuffin said, climbing shakily to his feet. "No thanks to you."

"Then walk," he ordered.

McGuffin staggered painfully after the fast-moving cop, across the parking lot to an unmarked car. He sat in the front seat and lay his head back as Chan started the car and jerked violently forward.

"Where are you takin' me?" McGuffin mumbled.

"To a hospital. You look awful."

"I wouldn't look so bad if you had done your job," McGuffin said.

"Protecting you is not my job," Chan replied. "I warned you to stay away from Mahoud, but you wouldn't listen."

"Why are you protecting Mahoud?" McGuffin demanded, lifting his head off the back of the seat. Things were hazy, but they seemed to be approaching Wilshire Boulevard.

"I'm not protecting anybody," Chan answered, unperturbed. He slowed, then ran the light on Wilshire, making a left turn and heading east.

"I want him arrested," McGuffin said.

"What for?" Chan asked, moving quickly through traffic, passing on the left and right.

"What for?" McGuffin exclaimed. "The sonofabitch tried to kill me!"

"You got any witnesses?"

"I'm the witness, that's all the witness I need!"

"Not in my jurisdiction," Chan answered.

"You sonofabitch," McGuffin muttered, sliding down in the front seat. Chan would do nothing. If he wanted satisfaction, he would have to go to the district attorney. And he would.

Chan turned at Westwood, wound through the Disneyland architecture until McGuffin thought he would be sick, then stopped finally in the parking lot at the UCLA Medical Center.

"There's the emergency room," Chan said, pointing out the doorway some fifty yards away.

"Thanks for nothin'," McGuffin said, reaching for the door handle.

"Just a minute," Chan said, laying a heavy hand on McGuffin's arm.

"I have to see the doctor, remember?"

"You'll go when I say you can go," Chan said, tightening his grip. McGuffin let go of the handle and sat back. "I know how it feels to be shot at," Chan assured him, as he felt for his cigarettes with his free hand. He found a crumpled pack atop the dash, removed the last one, and dropped the wrapping on the floor. "It makes you angry, it makes you want to get the motherfucker. But I can't have you doing that,

McGuffin. There are things going on that I can't have you
fucking up, so I'm warning you for the last time—lay off
Mahoud."

"Or what?" McGuffin asked. Chan was right, being shot
at makes you angry, angry enough to defy a mean cop.

Chan struck a match and lit his cigarette. He held the
match in the air, waited until the flame was close to his
fingers, then blew it out.

"Don't be a pest," he said.

"I don't understand cops like you," McGuffin said. "Two
people are dead and I was almost the third—all because
you won't move on Mahoud!"

"You don't know that Mahoud killed those people," Chan
said, throwing the match to the floor. "As a matter of fact,
you don't know one-half of what you think you know!"

"I know why Volper and Wenner were killed. You want
to hear it?"

"No."

"Fine, I'll tell you. Volper was selling coke to the movie
people for Mahoud. I should have known it when I saw that
five-million-dollar house—art films don't pay that well.
That's why Mahoud didn't mind losing a few million on
Volper's pictures. That was just a minor expense, compared
to the profit he was making."

"You think one coke dealer can turn that much profit?"
Chan scoffed.

"There are others, Wenner was one of them—probably
the whole Bronx Social Club—"

"Bullshit!" Chan said, sticking the cigarette into the corner of his mouth. When he squinted, one side of his face
folded up like an accordion. "Mahoud has an effective sales
force in place and now he's going around killing them?
Where's the profit in that?"

"He's killing them because somebody is holding out,"
McGuffin explained. Why couldn't the cop see it? He wasn't
stupid. "Somebody is holding Mahoud's coke and Mahoud
is going to go on killing until he finds it. Anybody who was
involved with Volper is in danger of being killed—Hoch-

man, Stein, Drumm, Judy Sloan, Jenny Lang—everybody. Unless you do something!"

Chan blew a great cloud of smoke against the windshield and shook his head slowly. "I can't do anything about it."

"You mean won't!" McGuffin charged. "People are gonna be killed and you sit here doing nothing! Why, for God's sake?"

Their eyes met and, in an instant, McGuffin knew. Pedro Chan wanted that package of coke for himself. Chan wasn't a lazy cop, he was a renegade cop, off on a lark of his own. He wanted Mahoud to kill me, McGuffin realized. That's why he didn't go to Mahoud's place when he knew I was going there. But Mahoud failed and now, McGuffin realized, staring into Chan's cold black eyes, the cop would have to do it himself.

"So that's why," McGuffin said softly. "You want that package for yourself."

Chan said nothing as he dabbed his cigarette out in the ashtray. Then he threw his arm over the back of the seat, exposing his detective special on his belt. He pointed to the emergency room. "I think you oughtta see a doctor," he said.

McGuffin looked across the parking lot at the emergency entrance. It was a long sprint in his condition, more than long enough for a cop to shoot a fleeing prisoner. McGuffin didn't move.

"What are you waiting for?" Chan asked. "You don't think I'd kill you, do you?"

McGuffin nodded. "Yeah, I think you would," he said, as he reached slowly for the door handle. "So much so, in fact, that I'm going to walk backward to the emergency room, with my hands in the air. You could still shoot me," he said, as he slowly opened the door and stuck one foot out, "but you'll have a hell of a time explaining a fleeing prisoner running backward with his hands in the air."

He was out of the car, backing slowly toward the emergency door, when Chan leaned across the seat and grabbed the door handle. "Go get your face fixed, McGuffin. I want you to look pretty at your wake," he said, then slammed the car door shut.

McGuffin stood, hands in the air, as Chan headed across the parking lot for the street in a broad squealing arc. A nurse crossing the lot, seeing the bloodied man in the torn suit with his hands raised, approached curiously.

"Have you had an accident?" she asked.

McGuffin lowered his hands. "Not yet," he answered.

Knowing from past experience the aches and pains that awaited him the next day, McGuffin hoped to be able to sleep until noon. But that was not to be. At a little after nine he was summoned by the jangling of the phone to an excruciating awareness of never-seen and long-unused muscles that cried out to be left alone. His greeting was an unintelligible, anguished groan.

"This is Mr. Worthy, of Executive Rent-A-Car," the caller informed him.

"Oh, yeah," McGuffin remembered. He had been wondering what to do about the car he had left at Mahoud's.

"I don't know how, but you apparently somehow managed to rent another car from our company," he began calmly.

"Yeah, I was going to call you about—" McGuffin started to explain.

"Which car has been found by the police," Worthy interrupted. "At the bottom of a cliff off Mulholland Drive."

"So that's what they did with it," McGuffin said.

"That's what who did with it, Mr. McGuffin?" Worthy was a model of corporate reserve.

"The Arabs," McGuffin answered.

"Arabs," he repeated dully. "Not surfers this time?"

"No, Arabs," McGuffin insisted.

"Perhaps they were Arab surfers."

"No, just Arabs."

"I don't understand you, Mr. McGuffin," Worthy said, a faint, plaintive note creeping into his voice. "You rent a car from us, you pound it beyond recognition, then you dump it into the ocean. You rent another and you push it off a cliff. Tell me, Mr. McGuffin—because by now I'm geniunely curious—what possible thrill can there be in this for you?"

"No thrill, Mr. Worthy," McGuffin assured him, "just a strange series of coincidences."

"Coincidences," he repeated calmly. "And that, I take it, is all the excuse you are going to offer?"

"I could tell you the whole story," McGuffin offered. "But I don't think you'd believe it."

"Try me," the executive suggested.

"Well, yesterday I went up to see these Arabs in Bel Air," McGuffin began. "They knocked me out and dragged me down to the wine cellar and then they poured wine down my throat—Lafite-Rothschild; and—"

The phone went dead in McGuffin's ear.

"I told you you wouldn't believe me," McGuffin said, replacing the receiver.

Painfully, he pulled himself out of bed and into the bathroom, then he stood before the full-length mirror, surveying the abrasions and contusions to his face and body. His hands and knees were scraped, the head wound had taken several stitches, his face was deeply scratched, and in several places blue bruises hung on his white skin like storm clouds. Not very pretty, he decided, rubbing his stubbled cheek. Shaving would be a bitch. But I look a hell of a lot better than my suit, he thought, seeing it in a pile on the bathroom floor, where he had stripped it off the night before. It was torn and bloodstained and both knees were gone—not even fit for a scarecrow. He would have to charge Volpersky for a new suit.

After a shower and a light breakfast in the coffee shop (where the counterman asked McGuffin if he was a stunt man), he wandered into the men's shop, wearing his extra flannel slacks and a dress shirt. The clerk, who was arranging ties on a rack, as if decorating a Christmas tree, regarded the wounded man with some apprehension.

"Something I can do for you?" the clerk asked.

"Yeah, I need a new jacket," McGuffin said. "Something

lightweight that'll go with these pants."

The clerk cupped his chin and elbow and studied his problem. "How about something in a blue blazer?" he suggested, reaching for a coat.

"Yeah, fine," McGuffin said. He hadn't owned a blue blazer since last Saint Patrick's Day, when Judge Brennan threw up all over him in the back of a cab.

McGuffin winced and groaned audibly when he bent low to slip into the offered jacket.

"Automobile accident?" the clerk inquired.

"Aviation," McGuffin said, studying himself in the mirror. The jacket would do, he decided. "How much is it?"

"I believe that's five hundred," the clerk said, consulting the sleeve. "Yes, five hundred. The wool is six."

"Oh, you have wool!" McGuffin exclaimed, slipping quickly out of the cotton jacket and thrusting it at the clerk. "Let me bring my wife by later," he pleaded, backing toward the door. "I'll let her decide."

The clerk shrugged and returned the coat to stock as his battered customer backed through the door and fled down the hall.

"Five hundred dollars for a lousy sport jacket," McGuffin mumbled as he hurried through the lobby. He could get a suit at Kirk's for half that.

He stopped at the desk to pick up his messages. There was one from Nat Volpersky, but nothing else. He went to the pay phone in the lobby and placed a collect call to Volpersky in New York.

"Yes, I'll accept!" Volpersky anxiously interrupted the operator. "So, Mr. McGuffin, what's wrong? On my money you go to some fancy hotel in Hollywood and I don't hear anymore from you. What's going on?"

"I'm sorry, Mr. Volpersky, things have been hectic," McGuffin apologized.

"Hectic I'm sure. What's the matter? You don't sound so good."

"I'm fine—a little under the weather, that's all."

"You've been drinking?"

"No." The extenuating circumstances were too complicated for anything other than a lie. "I got roughed up yesterday."

"By who?"

"An Arab."

"So welcome to the club. What's this got to do with my Ben?"

"I don't know yet," McGuffin lied again. "Tell me, Mr. Volpersky, if Ben wanted to hide out from somebody, is there anyplace where he might go that you know about—a cabin at the lake, or something like that?"

"A cabin at the lake? What, are you meshugge? That's for the goyim. Me, I got a cabana at the Bronx Beach Club. Anyway, why should Ben want to hide out from somebody? He hasn't done anything wrong, has he, Mr. McGuffin?"

"No, he hasn't done anything wrong," McGuffin said.

"And you're still looking for him?"

"Yeah, I'm still looking for him. By the way, I'm afraid I'm going to have to send you a bill for a new suit," McGuffin remembered.

"Suit?" Volpersky exclaimed. "I gotta buy your clothes yet?"

"I'll explain it all in my report," McGuffin promised.

"Never mind explaining, I trust you—too dumb to steal—just tell me how much."

"About two hundred and fifty dollars," McGuffin estimated.

"Two hundred fifty?" Mr. Volpersky exclaimed. "For one suit? I don't pay that much for my cars! What size are you?"

"Forty-two long. Why?"

"Pants?"

"Thirty-five, but I intend to lose a couple of inches—"

"Inseam?"

"I don't know—long. But listen, Mr. Volpersky, I don't want you to trouble yourself—"

"It's no trouble, believe me. Two hundred fifty dollars for one suit! It must be made with gold thread yet. Listen, you find my Ben, you let me worry about the suit."

McGuffin's protest fell on deaf ears. His suit, with two

pairs of pants yet, would be arriving by Air Express first thing in the morning.

"Damn," McGuffin grumbled, as he hung up the phone. He was very particular about his clothes—he liked them all to look alike.

Standing at the phone, comfortably contemplating his bland wardrobe, he looked across the lobby at the colorfully plumed actor skipping athletically up the front stairs and through the front doors. It was Mark Drumm, in the sort of white coveralls expensive mechanics used to wear, now called jump suits and often seen on expensive women. Drumm's male version had macho zippers everywhere except in front, which fell open from neck to navel, revealing a broad expanse of suntanned, hairy chest and enough jewelry to require a gold-chain snatcher to make two trips. He wore leather driving gloves, which he was busy peeling off as he crossed the lobby, almost bumping into McGuffin, as the detective put himself between Drumm and the Polo Lounge.

"Mr. Drumm?"

"Well, Mr. McGuffin," Drumm said, stopping and pushing his Porsche glasses atop his black curly hair. "You look like you stumbled into the lion's cage."

"I'd like to talk to you."

"I have an important meeting," Drumm said, glancing at his watch.

"Not with Aba Ben Mahoud, I hope," McGuffin said, moving into the actor's path as he started for the lounge.

"I don't know that that's any of your business," Drumm informed him.

"You know, Drumm, it wouldn't make any more difference to me than it would to the movie industry if Mahoud were to blow you away, but professional ethics require that I warn you—Mahoud is looking for something and he's going to kill anybody who might know where it is. And I think that includes you."

"What are you saying, McGuffin?" the actor asked warily.

"I think you were one of Ben Volper's drug runners, just

like Victor Wenner, who's probably dead by now; and you might be too, unless somebody comes up with that missing package of coke very soon."

"You're saying I'm a drug dealer?" Drumm asked, blinking furiously, ready, McGuffin could see, to explode.

McGuffin smiled. "And I thought actors were dumb."

Drumm glanced around the lobby, then leaned close to McGuffin. "Do me a favor, McGuffin. The next time we meet, pick a lonely place where I'll be free to kick your face in."

"I wish you wouldn't," McGuffin said. "I've been knocked around enough for one job. Now let's not bullshit each other, you're up to your ass in cocaine and if you don't get out, you're gonna be buried in it, along with Stein and Hochman and everybody else who's involved."

Drumm stepped back, the belligerence gone suddenly from his face. "You think Mahoud killed Vic?" he asked.

"Either Mahoud or a certain cop I know. There are too many bad guys in this movie, Drumm. You can't grab the drapes and swing out the castle window. So tell me where that package is before somebody else gets killed."

The movie star shook his head and looked away. "I can't."

"Why? Because others are involved?" Drumm looked at him but said nothing. "Tell me who they are, I'll talk to them."

"I can't—I can't name others." Drumm protested.

"Damn it, Drumm, this isn't a witch hunt. It's a drug war. People are going to be killed if you don't help!" Guests passing through the lobby were walking slowly and staring at them, but McGuffin couldn't let up. If Drumm would tell him where the package was, he could get it past Chan, to the district attorney's office, and end the killing.

"I don't want to talk about this now," Drumm said, trying to push past McGuffin.

"When?" McGuffin demanded, holding him.

"Maybe later—maybe never," he said, twisting away.

McGuffin had lost him; there was no sense going after him. But there were others who knew about the package— somebody would get scared, somebody would talk. He would just have to keep leaning until he found the soft spot.

In the meantime there was one more phone call to be made. He returned to the pay phone and waited while a kid with frizzy hair tried to convince a guy named Barney that no truly sensitive director works for less than a million dollars. Apparently Barney was not convinced. When the kid left, exasperated, McGuffin dropped a dime into the phone and dialed Information.

"The district attorney's office," McGuffin instructed.

While he waited, David Hochman and Isaac Stein entered the lobby, followed a moment later by Judy Sloan, trailing cigarette smoke and wispy blond hair. Hochman seemed pale and tense. He waited for the agent to catch up, then put himself between her and the director, as if he required their support as they strode toward the Polo Lounge.

McGuffin was about to call out to them, when he thought better of it. Let Drumm tell them that he knew they were dealing drugs as well as holding out on Mahoud, and that unless somebody came up with that package of dope, Mahoud was going to kill them all, one by one. Let that sink in first, McGuffin decided. Then he would speak to them one at a time. And David Hochman, he decided, watching as the writer disappeared between agent and director, would be first.

"District attorney's office," a female voice at the other end of the line informed him.

"Oh, yeah..." McGuffin said. He had forgotten whom he was calling.

Later that afternoon McGuffin told his story to a young assistant district attorney named Rosen, who sat in his shirt sleeves, glancing at his watch, as McGuffin registered his complaint about Pedro Chan. McGuffin too was in shirt sleeves, not yet having had time to buy a jacket. McGuffin explained the events that had led him here, just the way lawyers like to hear it, without any adjectives. He charged that Chan was a renegade cop, too busy looking for Mahoud's cocaine to arrest him for A and B or attempted murder.

"It sounds like you had a lot to drink up there," the young lawyer said, when McGuffin had finished the harrowing tale of his narrow escape.

It occurred to McGuffin that Assistant District Attorney Rosen thought he was a kook.

"It might seem like a lot to you, kid, but not to me," McGuffin replied testily.

"Okay," Rosen said, tossing his legal pad up on the desk and leaning back in his chair to reveal sweat-stained armpits. "If Pedro Chan is looking for the dope and Mahoud is looking for the dope, why won't Chan bust him just to get him out of the hunt?"

"Because Mahoud has a better chance of finding it than Chan does—he knows all of Volper's people. And when he does find it, Chan will be there to take it away from him."

Rosen nodded noncommittally. "And what proof do you have that Ben Volper was selling dope for"—he consulted the legal pad—"Aba Ben Mahoud?"

"I have Mark Drumm's admission, in the form of a failure to deny a direct charge. I know, I know," McGuffin added, when Rosen rolled his eyes at the ceiling. "But I also have Victor Wenner's girl friend, who will testify that Wenner was dealing drugs for Volper and Volper was being supplied by Mahoud."

"Hearsay," he said, and drew a line through Erin Green's name.

McGuffin was becoming annoyed. "I didn't know that I was going to be held to the rules of evidence, counselor. All I want to do is show sufficient cause to investigate Pedro Chan for corruption and I've done it."

"Yeah, maybe," Rosen agreed grudgingly, throwing his pen after the yellow pad.

"Then what's the problem?"

"Pedro Chan is the problem. I just can't believe he's protecting this Mahoud guy."

"Can't believe?" McGuffin was incredulous. "Kid, how long have you been out of law school?"

"Long enough to know that Chan's a straight cop," Rosen replied irritably.

"Kid, all crooked cops were at one time straight." He either didn't know he was annoying the lawyer, or he didn't care. "Maybe he changed his mind. Maybe he decided that being straight is a mug's game and he'd make one big score before retiring. Or maybe I'm making all this up because Chan threatened to kill me. But I intend to be heard—if not by the district attorney's office, then by the *Los Angeles Times*!"

"What did you say?" Rosen asked, suddenly interested.

"I said I'm going to the Times."

"No, about Chan threatening to kill you."

"When he drove me to the emergency room. He asked if I thought he was going to kill me and I said yeah, I knew he would. Then he told me to go see the doctor so I'd look pretty at my wake."

"Why didn't you tell me that in the first place?" he said, going for the phone.

"Christ, I told you everything else—" McGuffin said.

"About drugs. That's not a fashionable item. But police brutality! All across the country L.A. is choke-hold city. A D.A. can make a rep on that," he exclaimed. Then, into the phone: "Get me Fitzgerald, it's urgent!" He spoke to McGuffin while he waited for Fitzgerald. "How 'bout first thing Monday morning?"

"Fine."

Politics, McGuffin decided, as he was walking out of the building, was something he would never understand.

12

McGuffin was lying on the bed, fully dressed (except for the jacket, which he still hadn't bought), thinking that it had been a pretty good day. He hadn't found Ben Volper and he wouldn't, but he had started the machinery that might put a crooked cop and a major cocaine supplier away for a long time, and that felt good. The thing that bothered him was having to tell Nat Volpersky that his son had been a dope dealer and now he was dead. He would do it when the time came—he always had—but for now he would put it out of his mind. He would stare at the reflected porch light on the ceiling and listen to the faint sound of music coming from the ballroom. Stray words from "Tea for Two" buzzed into his head like flies that couldn't be swatted away.

On cue, the phone rang. It was Erin Green.

"The police found Vic's car at the airport," she said.

"What about Vic?" McGuffin asked, switching the bedside lamp on.

"No Vic, just his car," she answered. "But that could be a good sign, don't you think? I mean maybe he just got a little crazy and took a plane someplace." She was giddy with hope.

Or a little scared, McGuffin thought. "Yeah, maybe," he said, with little conviction.

"Only one thing worries me," she said, suddenly sober.

"What's that?"

"The inside of the car is all messed up—like somebody went through it looking for something."

"Oh, shit," McGuffin said.

"Is something wrong?"

"Where are you?" he asked.

"I'm at the airport. They said I can take Vic's car home, but I need somebody to drive mine."

"Who said you could take the car? Are the cops there now?" McGuffin asked, throwing his feet on the floor.

"No, there was nobody here. A cop called and told me where the car was. I had to walk all over the long-term parking lot looking for the goddamned thing and then—"

"Erin, the voice, the cop who called—what did he sound like?"

"I don't know—he sounded like a cop, that's all."

"Was it a high voice?" McGuffin pressed.

"Yeah, a little on the high side," she allowed.

"Listen to me, Erin," McGuffin spoke gravely. "Never mind Vic's car. Get in your own car and drive directly to the Beverly Hills Hotel. Do not go back to your own apartment, don't go anywhere near it. Do you understand?"

"Yeah, I understand," she said softly. "That guy who called—he wasn't a cop?"

"No, he wasn't a cop," McGuffin said. "I'll leave my key at the desk. You wait inside the bungalow and don't open the door to anybody but me," he ordered.

"Okay," she agreed. "But where are you going?"

"To your place, to pick up a package."

If somebody hasn't beaten me to it, he added to himself as he quickly hung up and got to his feet. The automatic was conspicuous in his pants pocket, so he covered it with a newspaper as he hurried out of the bungalow.

The desk clerk nodded knowingly when McGuffin hurriedly explained that a young woman would soon be arriving. He wanted to straighten him out, but there was no time. He hurried out the door and down the stairs, calling for his car—an Avis this time.

When the car arrived, McGuffin exchanged places with the driver with the efficiency of a relay runner, then raced down the hill and across Sunset on a changing amber light. Navigating from memory—he had left his map in the last car—he managed to get to Hollywood without any mishap. He parked illegally in front of the building and rushed up the stairs to the lobby. He could ring all the bells and talk his way in, or jimmy the lock with his American Express card, depending upon the lock. One look at the lock decided the matter. He was inside in only a few seconds. It was the first time, he mused, as he moved quickly and quietly across the lobby, that he had used his defunct American Express card in several months.

He paused at the bottom of the stairs and listened. Hearing nothing, he removed the automatic from his side pocket and started slowly and cautiously up the stairs. On the second floor a television was playing and on the third someone was frying hamburger and onions, but these were the only signs of life in the building. The green door on the top floor was closed and no light issued from around or under it.

McGuffin stood with his ear at the door for a full minute, then shifted the gun to his left hand and tried the knob with his right. It turned and the door came open a fraction of an inch. He let it close, then tiptoed back to the bare light bulb over the stairs. Standing on his toes, he could just reach it. A few quick turns of the hot bulb and the hall was almost totally black.

He made his way back to the green door by memory, opened it, and quietly slipped inside. He crouched, motionless, in the dark, gun at the ready, and waited for somebody to move. After nearly a minute, when he had just about decided it was safe to move, he heard a faint sound from deep within the black room. He crouched lower and lower, until he was lying flat on his stomach, gun extended in front of him in two hands, waiting for the light, ready to shoot anything that moved. He heard the sound again, closer this time, like something soft brushing against a drum. When something furry brushed against his hand, McGuffin leaped to his feet (he might have shouted, but he would never remember), accompanied by an inhuman shriek, and fumbled for the light switch next to the door. Finding the light, he also found a black cat, no less frightened than McGuffin, standing in the middle of the room, its back arched like a Halloween cat.

"Jesus..." McGuffin breathed.

The cat meowed. There was no one else in the room, but someone had been there. Film cans and unraveled spools of film were strewn knee-deep over the floor, along with clothes and linens—even the food from the refrigerator.

"It's all right," McGuffin told the cat, as he put his gun away. The celluloid sounded like dried corn husks as he walked through it. The cat watched as McGuffin poked through the loft, decided he was at least a safer bet than whoever had just been there, and came forward to rub against his leg. There was little reason to look around—he had no way of knowing if the coke had been taken, or even if it had been there, although that was McGuffin's suspicion. Who got it? McGuffin wondered. Mahoud or Chan?

"I don't suppose you can talk," he said to the cat. The cat looked up and meowed. "Useless animals," McGuffin complained, as he turned and thrashed through the film to the door.

The cat meowed again as McGuffin started to close the door. He considered for a moment, then bent down and picked it up.

"Come on, I'll take you to your mistress," he said, resting the black, furry thing against his side.

On the ride back, the cat climbed up on his lap and purred contentedly.

"At least one of us is happy about all this," McGuffin said to the cat.

He parked on the street and carried the purring cat to the bungalow. He didn't know how the management felt about pets or, for that matter, about unregistered female guests.

He knocked lightly on the door.

"Mr. McGuffin?" Erin inquired from the other side.

"Yeah, open up."

She opened the door and McGuffin slipped in, tossing the cat on the bed.

"I brought you your cat," he said.

She looked at the cat, then at McGuffin. "My cat?"

"Isn't this your cat?"

"I've never seen this cat before in my life," she said.

"But I found him in your apartment."

"I can't help it, he's not mine. I've never owned a cat in my entire life. I hate cats. I'd own a king cobra before I'd own a cat."

"Hmm," McGuffin said, looking at the cat. The cat lay on the bed, cocking his head first at one, then at the other of them. "Then how do you suppose he got into your loft?"

"I have no idea."

"Hmm," McGuffin repeated. "You don't like cats at all?"

"I despise them."

"Then what am I going to do with him?" he asked.

"Throw him out," she said.

"I couldn't do that," McGuffin said.

The cat continued to look back and forth at them while his fate was being debated.

"Well, don't think you're going to give him to me," she told him.

"Okay," McGuffin agreed. He would worry about the cat later. When he removed the gun from his pocket, she gasped.

"You're not going to shoot it!"

"What? Oh," McGuffin said, becoming aware of the gun in his hand. "Yeah, I'm afraid I'll have to."

"You can't do that!" she protested, wide-eyed with fright.

"What else can I do if nobody wants him?" he asked helplessly. "I can't put him out on the street to starve."

"You could give him to the ASPCA," she proposed.

McGuffin shook his head sadly. "They'd only put him to sleep. There's no dignity in that. Let him go out the honorable way—with a slug in the head."

She stared incredulously as McGuffin sat on the bed and pressed the muzzle against the cat's ear. When he looked away and slowly drew the hammer back, she gasped: "I'll take it!"

McGuffin smiled and carefully lowered the hammer as

she snatched the cat from under the gun. She sat on the bed and pressed the cat to her, as if she feared this madman might have a change of heart.

"Any man who would shoot a cat..." she mumbled.

McGuffin stuffed his gun in his belt and tried to sound like Humphrey Bogart. "It's a dirty job, but somebody's gotta do it." Not bad. But Erin didn't seem to pick up on it, so he tried again. "All you nice respectable people, you want the streets free of stray cats, but you don't wanna know how it's done."

"That's the worst imitation of Lauren Bacall I've ever heard," she said.

"Yeah, but you fell for the gun and the cat bit," McGuffin said.

"Bastard," she said, still stroking the cat. He was beginning to purr loudly.

"He likes you," McGuffin said. He removed the gun from his belt and dropped it in the bag beside the statue of the Virgin. "Unlike whoever broke into your apartment tonight. I'm afraid they made a mess of things."

She continued to stroke the cat while McGuffin described the condition of her apartment. "Why would they want to trash our place?" she asked. "We've got nothing in there but some editing equipment."

"They weren't looking for editing equipment, that's still there. They were looking for cocaine, a very large package of cocaine." McGuffin leaned over and turned her face to his. "Tell me the truth, Erin—did they find it?"

She shook her head. "If Vic had it, he didn't have it there."

"You told me before that he kept bags of the stuff in the apartment," he reminded her.

"*Small* bags," she corrected. "Just enough for his own use."

"Worth how much?"

"A thousand dollars—maybe two—no more than that," she assured him.

"If he had more—a package worth several million dollars—where would he keep it?"

"Several million!" She gasped. "Vic never—"

"If he did," McGuffin interrupted. "Where would he hide it?"

"I don't know," she answered.

"You're not doing Vic any good by holding out on me, you know. I'm trying to help."

"I'm not holding out," she said, her eyes watering.

McGuffin believed her. "Okay," he said, backing off and standing erect. He rolled his shoulders against the soreness that had settled in his back.

"What happened to you?" she asked, staring at his scratched face.

"I dived through a stained-glass window and off a cliff," he answered.

"That's a tough act to follow."

"I hope I don't have to. Tell me about Victor's business," he demanded abruptly.

"Directing?"

"Drugs. He and Volper were selling and Mahoud was supplying. Right?"

"Right," she answered, slowly nodding.

"Who else was involved?"

"Shit," she answered. "Why don't you ask me who wasn't?"

"You?"

She thought about it for a moment. "Yeah, I guess so."

"You guess so!"

"I mean I delivered the shit and I collected the money and I got to keep a little for myself. Does that make me a pro?"

"I'm sure it at least jeopardizes your amateur status," McGuffin replied.

"But I didn't do it for the money—none of us did. I did it so I could cut Ben's picture, Victor so he could direct, and Ben did it to get financing from Mahoud. It was a way to make films, that's all. If we didn't do it, somebody else would have."

"Yeah, and somebody else would be dead instead of Ben Volper," McGuffin replied. He had been about to include

Victor Wenner, but caught himself. He needn't have. He could tell from the expression on her face that she knew she had gone from the amateur ranks to the pros in the last twenty-four hours.

"Do you have some place to stay?" he asked her.

Her answer was barely audible. "No." A tear broke and ran down her cheek. The cat, oblivious to everything but her rubbing, was purring, eyes closed.

"You can have that bed," McGuffin said.

Later, when they were in bed, she in his last clean shirt, and long after McGuffin thought she was sleeping, she spoke with a clear, dry voice in the darkness. "Mr. McGuffin?"

"Yes?"

"Is Victor dead?"

McGuffin was slow to answer. "I don't know."

A little while later she asked: "Can I get in bed with you?"

Again McGuffin was slow to answer.

"Nothing fancy," she said. "I just don't want to be alone."

McGuffin lifted the light blanket and she crawled in next to him. She threw an arm around his waist and pressed her lanky body against his back. He felt a shudder and realized that she was crying. She reminded him of his daughter when she used to crawl into bed with him and her mother after a bad dream. He wanted to put his arm around Erin and tell her it was only a bad dream, but she was too old for that. It would also be difficult to turn and face her in his present state.

He needn't have worried. A moment later she slid her hand down his body and the cat was out of the bag. Her head followed almost instantly.

"I want you to know," she said, pausing to look up at McGuffin, "this is only therapy."

13

McGuffin was awakened the next morning by something soft and furry pressing against his face. He opened his free eye—Erin was asleep beside him, her head resting on his shoulder—and the cat was sleeping between them. Trying not to wake her, he picked the cat up with one hand and tossed it off the bed. It came back like a yo-yo.

"Shoo—go away!" McGuffin whispered, pushing against the resistant cat. "Not you," he said, when Erin sighed and rolled over to the edge of the bed.

Neither asleep nor fully awake, she returned to her place beside him, wrapping an arm and a leg around him while seeking a comfortable position against his chest, like a nursing baby. Beaten, the cat retired to the foot of the bed to sulk and meow irritably. McGuffin was amazed at how easily both of them, the cat and the girl, had adjusted to the sudden loss and change in their lives. Her intended husband disappears—is killed—and scarcely a day later, here she is in bed with me! No more loyalty than a cat; she'll go with anybody who'll stroke her and give her a meal. At the thought of food, it occurred to him why the cat was complaining.

"Erin, are you awake?" he asked, shaking her.

"No."

"Your cat is hungry."

"*My* cat?" she exclaimed, coming fully awake.

"You agreed to take it," McGuffin reminded her.

"It wasn't fair," she protested, as McGuffin pushed her out of bed.

He was surprised, when he watched her walk naked into the bathroom, at how much fuller she looked undressed than dressed. She was one of those women who are entirely relaxed in their nakedness—or perhaps that was common to her generation. No romance, these kids.

"Goddamn!" she wailed from the bathroom.

"What's the matter?"

"The cat shit in the bathtub!"

"It's your cat," McGuffin reminded her.

After hearing some muttering, he heard the toilet flush, followed by the sound of the shower. When she emerged, her skin glowed pink and her hair was damp at the edges.

"I used your toothbrush," she said, as she slipped into the same clothes she had worn last night.

"Okay," McGuffin said. That was another familiarity of this generation he was unable to abide. A toothbrush, for Christ's sake! What was more intimate than a toothbrush?

"I'll need some money," she said.

McGuffin got out of bed and walked across the room to his pants, hanging from the back of a chair, as someone knocked on the door. Erin pulled the door open before McGuffin could protest.

"Air Express," the young man on the porch said, staring at McGuffin, naked except for the pair of pants he held in front of himself.

"My suit!" McGuffin remembered.

"I hope so," the young man said, handing the box to Erin.

McGuffin found two singles in his pocket, which he passed to the delivery man. Erin signed for the package, handed the Air Express man the receipt, and closed the door.

"I'll need some money for cat food," she said.

"I thought this was *your* cat," McGuffin complained, pulling a ten-dollar bill from his pocket.

"Where do I get cat food at the Beverly Hills Hotel?" she asked, ignoring this.

McGuffin shrugged. "At the coffee shop?"

"What—doughnuts and coffee?"

"A tuna sandwich—or liverwurst—use your imagination. And milk, cats like milk."

"Yeah, I seem to remember that," she said, as she closed the door after her.

Left alone, McGuffin went to the package on the bed to see what kind of suit Nat Volpersky had picked out for him. It was blue with wide pinstripes, he saw when he turned back the tissue, and rather shiny, as if it had been ironed. He held the jacket at arm's length and considered. It had wide lapels and it was blocky, not at all tailored at the waist—but maybe that was just the way it looked when held at arm's length. It was certainly not the kind of suit he would have picked, but if he could just make do with it until he got back to San Francisco....He tossed it on the bed and went into the bathroom for a shower.

He was putting the last touches to his tie when Erin returned with the cat's breakfast.

"Oh my God."

"What?" McGuffin said, turning to face her.

She walked around him, as if she were studying a statue in an art museum, something strange and modern—or perhaps outrageously old-fashioned.

"Type-fucking-casting!" she exclaimed, with what sounded like approval.

"You like it?"

"Like it? You look like Humphrey Bogart!"

"Come on—"

"I mean 19-fucking-40s! All you need is the snap fedora and the wet cigarette. So that's why you have your suits sent from New York—there's some tailor back there where all the private eyes go, right? A little guy in the basement in the West Forties, a 1949 calendar on the wall and Sam Spade and the Thin Man and all these guys waiting to be fitted for a suit—right?"

"Okay, you've made your point," McGuffin said, removing the jacket and throwing it at the cat on the bed. "I'll blow five hundred on the blazer."

"Hey, wait, I was only kidding," she said, retrieving the

jacket from the bed. "The suit is perfect."

"You think so?" he asked, allowing her to put the jacket back on him.

"Absolutely. Especially for somebody in your line of work. I mean it lends authenticity," she added quickly, before he could protest.

Not thoroughly convinced, McGuffin studied himself in the full-length mirror. It was old-fashioned, that was true, but there was a certain Bogartish kind of validity to it, sort of. What the hell, he decided. I'll wear it until somebody laughs.

"I got chopped liver on rye and a carton of milk," she said, pulling the sandwich from the bag as the cat leaped from the bed and went for her legs, rubbing and purring. "Almost ten dollars. I tell you, this is no Horn & Hardart."

She poured the milk into an ashtray and put it on the floor for the cat, then scraped the chopped liver off the bread and onto the wrapping paper. The cat went from the milk to the chopped liver, then back to the milk, dizzy with pleasure.

"I suppose we should give him a name," she said, watching him eat.

"How about Aba Ben Mahoud?"

"Very toney."

"Then it's Aba Ben Mahoud."

When McGuffin walked across the room to where Erin knelt beside the feeding cat, she wrapped one arm around his leg and pressed against him. McGuffin reached down and stroked her red hair. When the cat finished eating, he came to her and rubbed against her leg.

"That cat's crazy about you," McGuffin observed.

"I kind of like him too," she said, trailing long, thin fingers over the cat's back.

"What are your plans?" McGuffin asked, after a moment.

He felt her shrug against his leg. "I don't know. Go home and clean up the apartment, I guess."

"I mean, what are your plans for the future?"

"I know what you meant." When she stopped stroking the cat, it moved back and forth under her hand, arching its back and meowing plaintively. "I had the feeling it was going to end badly with Vic. But I wasn't figuring on anything like this."

When McGuffin lifted her to her feet and kissed her lightly, she wrapped her arms tightly around him and pressed hard against him. He waited a long time before prying her loose.

"Come on, I'll take you home," he said.

The cat waited in her car while they ate lunch at a restaurant she knew that was on the way to her apartment. It was an Italian place, with poster-size pictures of several actors and actresses, most but not all Italian, gracing the barn-siding walls. McGuffin had three bottles of Calistoga water with his abalone scallopine and watched forlornly as the lanky girl downed half a bottle of Chianti with her baked ziti.

"I can't imagine a tough private eye who doesn't drink," she said, shaking the last drops from her bottle.

"Neither can I." McGuffin sighed.

Lunch finished, the two-car motorcade resumed, McGuffin following her to her apartment. They both parked in the same parking lot, diagonally across from her building, then walked together to her apartment. She carried the cat, while McGuffin fingered the automatic resting in the pocket of his new suit.

McGuffin took the key from her and opened the front door, then led the way to her apartment. He waited outside for a moment and listened, then pushed the door open and walked in. It was the same mess he had seen the night before. Erin walked to the center of the room, staring wide-eyed at the carnage, but saying nothing, then slowly placed the cat on the floor, in the exact spot where McGuffin had first seen him.

"What a dump," she said, then took a noisy step forward through the film that littered the floor. "Why would anyone want to do this? It's just film, not cocaine."

When she began to cry, McGuffin opened his arms and she pressed against him. He pried the lapel from under her, so that her tears would fall on his shirt. Since no one had gawked at his suit in the Italian restaurant, he was thinking of keeping it, even after he got back to San Francisco.

"They thought he was hiding it in the canisters," McGuffin guessed.

"You can tell it's film just by shaking it," she said, sobbing. "It's all the stuff we did together. Just look at the place! It's like they did it to me!" she cried.

"I know," McGuffin said, stroking and patting. "But it isn't you, it's just things. If you had been here, you'd be dead, but you're not. Remember that."

"Yeah, I know," she said, pulling away and rubbing her eyes with her knuckles. "It isn't much, but it's home." She turned from him and walked away, kicking at the film. The cat hopped quickly after her. "Even the food and the dishes," she said from the kitchen. "Why?"

"Maybe he got angry when he couldn't find it," McGuffin suggested. He followed her to the end of the room and stood surveying the mess. Food and ice had thawed and the water remained. The cat sniffed from one thing to the other, but found nothing to equal the Beverly Hills Hotel chopped liver. "Is there anyplace in the room where Vic might have hidden the stuff and they couldn't find it—a secret hiding place only the two of you know about?"

"No," she said too quickly, then remembered something.

"What is it?" McGuffin asked.

"The hole in the wall next to the mattress," she said. "But it's too small for anything like a big package of coke."

"Not if it was in small bags," McGuffin said, going to the sleeping alcove.

The contents of the drawers and the drawers themselves were strewn about the room, but the mattress was still firmly against the wall. He grabbed it at the foot and pulled it away from the wall. There was a hole at the baseboard no larger than his fist. He removed his jacket and dropped it on the mattress, then reached into the hole. It was only a few inches deep and a couple of feet wide between the studs. He found a soft plastic bag and a couple of loose papers, which he gathered together in one hand and pulled out.

"That's his stash," Erin said, from the doorway, of the white powder in the plastic bag.

It was several ounces of cocaine, scarcely the hundred or so pounds McGuffin was looking for. Besides this there was a savings account book from a New York bank, several Polaroid pictures of himself and Erin in the sex act—which she promptly snatched away—and a white envelope.

"What's that?" she asked, as McGuffin tore the envelope open.

"Negatives," he said, dumping a pile of filmstrips on the bed.

"Home movies," she said, holding one up to the light. "That's Judy Sloan."

"How can you tell?" McGuffin asked. There seemed to be several figures seated on a couch.

"The hair," she said. "It's been bleached so much it's invisible. And that's Mark Drumm—you can't mistake that profile. And those are definitely Jenny Lang's tits."

McGuffin picked up another filmstrip and held it against the light. Now he could recognize the figures on the film, or most of them.

"Who are the other two?" he asked, handing her the film.

"Isaac Stein and David Hochman," she said, holding the films side by side. "They were taken at Ben Volper's house; I recognize the mirror behind the couch."

"The Bronx Social Club," McGuffin said. "They must have been taken at different times," he surmised, examining another film against the overhead light. "Hochman and Stein are in some of the pictures, but not all of them."

"That doesn't mean anything," she said. "They could have stepped out of the picture for a few minutes. The difference between these two strips is only a matter of—maybe eight to twelve minutes," she calculated by some mysterious process.

"How do you know that?" McGuffin asked.

She pointed. "By these code numbers on the side of the film. Assume he was shooting at about twenty-four frames per second and you can tell by the difference in the numbers how much time has elapsed. These are just outtakes," she said, dropping the strips on the bed. "Somewhere there's a home movie—which Jenny Lang probably has—of the Bronx Social Club acting silly on the couch."

"But why would Victor have the outtakes in his secret hiding place?" McGuffin asked.

"You got me," she said. "I could put it together in the order it was shot and let you have a look at it if you think it's important," she offered. "But first I'd like to clean up this mess."

"Do it later," McGuffin said. "I don't think you should stay here alone."

"Don't worry about me," she said.

"I can't help it," McGuffin said, getting to his feet. She held his coat and he slipped into the sleeves.

"Nice suit," she said, as she walked him to the door.

McGuffin kissed her lightly. "Thanks. You're sure you want to stay here alone?"

"I'll be all right. But that doesn't mean I wouldn't like to see you again," she added.

"I'll call you," he promised, as he turned and walked to the stairs.

He didn't like leaving her there alone. Even if she didn't know anything, Mahoud or Chan—whoever had busted the place up—didn't know that, and he might come back to lean on her. But she knew that and still she was staying, and McGuffin admired her for it.

14

The filmstrips were nothing, McGuffin was sure, just the Bronx Social Club sitting on Volper's couch and acting foolish; but the fact that Victor had hidden them in the wall and not mentioned them to Erin was peculiar and at least worth a phone call to Jenny Lang. If the apparently innocuous outtakes were worth concealing, the completed reel might be worth viewing. And besides, it afforded him the opportunity to see Jenny Lang again.

Erin's right, McGuffin mused, as he turned west on Santa Monica Boulevard, Jenny Lang's tits were unmistakable, even under a thick sweater. Not that McGuffin was a breast man—he liked it all, and even when he was approaching—had entered?—middle age, sex was still a dazzling gift for which he considered himself still somehow unworthy. This attitude was the residue of his Catholic training, he knew. Would it never go away?

He pulled into a shopping mall on Santa Monica and called Jenny Lang, but got a busy signal, then got back into the car and continued on toward the ocean. There was a more efficient route to Malibu, he knew, but he dreaded the freeways. It seemed that such routes almost always involved a gas station attendant shaking his head sadly and pointing back, way back, in the direction from which he had come. On the Ocean Highway he stopped near the Chart House and placed a second call, but again the line was busy. Erin's phone had been off the hook when he entered her studio, McGuffin remembered, as he unconsciously hurried across the parking lot to his idling car. He raced along the side of the road, spitting sand and dust, then forced his way onto the highway over the angry protest of a honking motorist. Weaving recklessly in and out of traffic, he pushed the little car to ninety at times, managing somehow to make it to Malibu without a speeding ticket.

At the guard shack, McGuffin was again halted by the same guard, to await permission from the mistress of the manor.

"Phone's busy," the guard informed him.

"It's been busy for a long time, I'm afraid something may have happened," McGuffin informed him.

"Uh-huh." The guard nodded. He had heard it all, from the fans who wanted only an autograph to the writers who wanted only to get their script to a star, and it was all a matter of life and death.

McGuffin backed the car around in a fusillade of spitting gravel and headed back to the highway. This time he parked at the north end of the Colony, desiring no further confrontation with the south-side surfers, and hurried back along the beach, the automatic bouncing on his hip in his new Humphrey Bogart suit. He found the house, behind the high dune and back from the others, and hurried up onto the deck—then froze. The sliding glass was open, the curtain flapping, and strewn about the room were various articles of clothing—a shoe, a pair of jeans, a jacket. Someone had already been here, was perhaps even still inside.

Knowing and dreading what he was about to find, McGuffin withdrew the automatic from his pocket and forced himself forward. At the glass door, as he was about to step across the threshold, he stopped. It was scarcely audible— a groan from somewhere deep in the room, then another, from behind him this time. The solarium! He moved quickly and silently across the deck and, gun drawn, threw open the door.

It took only a split second to register, but the picture continued to play, like a slow-motion film, Jenny Lang astride a mount, a naked horsewoman, her voluptuous, sleekly oiled, brown body moving up and down, up and down, with the rhythm and energy of the rising and falling sea, accompanied by the slap of flesh on flesh, like splintering wood, as if the deck were breaking under each powerful thrust. McGuffin stared, transfixed, and she stared back, for what seemed many long seconds, until she screamed and dismounted in a headlong dive, crabbing about the floor for a towel or robe, while the head of her mount rose into view. It was Mark Drumm!

"You sonofabitch!" he screamed, grabbing the first thing that came to hand and throwing it across the deck.

It was a bottle of suntan oil and it caught McGuffin on the side of the head as he tried, unsuccessfully, to dodge it. Stunned, he hit the deck with a jarring force that dislodged the gun from his hand and sent it clattering across the cedar boards. This was followed by shouted curses and a second shattering jolt—Drumm's bare foot slamming at his chest. McGuffin curled up protectively, waiting for his breath to come and his head to clear, while above, a naked man tried to stomp him to death and a naked woman cried hysterically for him to stop.

Once, McGuffin managed to grab Drumm's ankle, but it was oily and slippery and he couldn't hold it. He could hear Jenny now, pleading with her lover, begging him to stop before he killed him. And he would kill him if he could, McGuffin was sure.

When he was ready, McGuffin came off the floor as if he were a racquet ball, catching Drumm in the midsection with his head, driving him across the deck, and slamming him against the wall. He went down in a heap, and Jenny threw herself on top of the actor before he could get back up.

"Get away!" he ordered, pushing at the naked woman as she tried to wrestle him to the floor.

"Stop it!" she screamed. "You'll kill him!"

McGuffin tested the bruise on his head and watched as the two naked, oil-slick wrestlers grappled futilely. Furious though he was, he was also amused—and becoming a little excited. Jenny Lang, "the most voluptuous woman in Hollywood," wrestling naked with matinee idol Mark Drumm. It would make one hell of a pornographic film. But Mark

Drumm, perfectionist that he was, wanted the ultimate in pornography—a snuff film.

McGuffin had forgotten about the gun. Drumm, in his thrashing, had probably discovered it only by accident, but now he had it. And contorted as he was, with Jenny Lang's strong legs wrapped around his neck, Drumm pointed the gun directly at McGuffin's chest.

McGuffin had the impression that Drumm had squeezed the trigger before Jenny fell on the gun, but he couldn't be sure. He managed to snatch the gun from beneath a pile of oily flesh and quickly whip the barrel twice across Drumm's head. It didn't render the actor totally unconscious—it wasn't meant to—but it would take the fight out of him for a while and leave him with a hell of a headache for a couple of days.

McGuffin looked at the safety catch above the trigger ring. It was up, the safety was on. Or did that mean it was off? He never could keep that straight. He pointed the gun out to sea and squeezed the trigger. It moved slightly, then froze. The safety had been on. He could scarcely believe that Drumm would try to shoot him just because he had interrupted his lovemaking. Still, he was thankful Jenny had fallen on him before Drumm was able to find the safety catch.

"Mark, are you all right?" Jenny asked, holding his face in her hands.

Only a couple of days ago it was my foot, McGuffin remembered. How soon they forget.

"He'll be okay," McGuffin assured her. "I didn't hit him half as hard as I should have."

"I'm sorry, Mark is excitable," she said. "But you had no right to burst in on us like that," she added.

"I'm sorry," McGuffin said. "I thought somebody was dying in here."

"You call this dying, you stupid fuck?" Drumm groaned, squirming to a sitting position.

"Mark!" Jenny Lang cautioned. "It was a mistake."

"Yeah, a mistake," McGuffin said, watching as she climbed to her feet. There were no bathing-suit marks anywhere on her oiled, tan body.

"So if you'd put that gun away—" She pointed.

"Right," McGuffin said. Up is on, down is off, he reminded himself as he dropped the gun into his pocket.

"And turn around?" She motioned.

McGuffin did as he was instructed.

"You can turn around now," she said.

When he did, both of them were wrapped from head to foot in white terry-cloth robes. Mark Drumm's had the initials BV on the pocket.

"He's a fucking lunatic," Drumm moaned, pressing a towel to his head. "Busting in on people with a gun. Haven't you ever heard of telephones?"

"I tried to phone," McGuffin answered. "But the phone was busy and I was worried that something had happened."

"The phone was busy so he got worried," Drumm said to no one.

"How long were you standing there, you creep?"

"Mark!" Jenny again warned.

"Only a second, just a split second," McGuffin assured them.

"Yeah, I'll bet," he snarled, snatching his cigarettes from the edge of the hot tub.

"I don't think we're entirely justified in being angry at Mr. McGuffin," she pointedly informed her lover. He only snorted and turned his back to McGuffin. "I hope you'll understand," she went on, talking to McGuffin, "that things aren't entirely what they seem." She made a fist with one hand and stared helplessly at her bare feet. They were brown and shiny with oil, like a well-seasoned baseball glove. "What happened just now, happened very suddenly. Out of—I don't know what—grief perhaps. I was feeling terribly alone and—"

"You don't have to explain to him," Mark Drumm put in, as he turned, the unlit cigarette dancing in the corner of his mouth. "He's got no business even being here."

"He's looking for Ben," Jenny Lang reminded him.

"He's spreading vicious rumors, that's all he's doin'," Drumm said, jabbing a finger at the detective. "Tell her what you told me at the Beverly Hills," he demanded, then

did so before McGuffin could reply. "He said Ben was dealing cocaine!"

She stared evenly at Drumm for a moment, then replied
softly: "And we both know he was."

"Jenny, for Christ's sake!" Drumm wailed.

"I think it's time we told Mr. McGuffin everything," she
said. "It can't hurt Ben now."

"No, and it might even help save some lives," McGuffin
put in.

Mark Drumm groaned and sat heavily on the step beside
the hot tub as Jenny began her story. It was not going to be
very different from Erin Green's story, McGuffin quickly
suspected. It all began innocently; Volper needed money
to finance his films and Mahoud needed a network of sales-
men in the lucrative movie colony.

"Every month he gave Ben more cocaine, a quota, and
Ben kept enlisting more and more people to sell for him."

"How many?" McGuffin interrupted.

"Perhaps a dozen," she answered, with a glance at Drumm.

"What are their names?" McGuffin asked, reaching for
pad and pen.

"No names," Drumm objected. "I told you that at the
hotel."

"Mark is right," she said. "I have no right to involve the
others."

"One of them may be holding a shipment of cocaine, Mrs.
Volper. That person's life is in danger," McGuffin explained.

"I know who they all are; I can warn them," Drumm said.
Wisps of steam were beginning to rise from the hot tub
behind him. Apparently they had intended a soak after the
sex, McGuffin decided. He attempted to persuade her to
give him the list of dealers, but she was politely adamant.
McGuffin knew he would have no influence over her while
Mark Drumm was present.

"Ben tried to quit Mahoud after his last film," she said,
staring forlornly at the steam that rose and fluttered away
in the ocean breeze. "But Mahoud wouldn't let him. Ben
was afraid he would kill him."

And so he did, McGuffin thought. But he said nothing. Instead he asked: "How much cocaine was Ben moving in a month?"

She looked at Drumm. "A couple of hundred pounds?" he said, shrugging.

At more than a hundred thousand a pound street value, that came to more than two million a month, McGuffin calculated roughly. Certainly more than enough to kill for.

"Did your husband try to hold out on Mahoud?" McGuffin asked.

"No," she replied firmly. Then, "Not that I know—" uncertainly.

"I've already asked her that," Drumm cut in. "If Ben was hiding a shipment of coke, he didn't confide in any of us."

"But if he did, where would he be likely to hide a couple of hundred pounds of coke?" McGuffin asked.

She shook her head. "I have no idea."

"Could Victor Wenner have hidden it for him?"

"Vic Wenner would have walked into the ocean for Ben," Mark Drumm answered, as he struck a match. When he exhaled smoke across the hot tub, it blended with the steam and dissipated in a roiling wrestling match.

"Or with him," McGuffin said.

"Do you think Victor was killed?" Jenny asked, clutching the robe tightly around her.

McGuffin nodded. "And your lives may be in danger too. Be careful," he warned.

"Thanks for nothing," Drumm said.

McGuffin understood. There was only so much one detective could do. He started for the gate, then remembered. "Did your husband ever make home movies of the Bronx Social Club?" he asked, turning to the actress.

"Often," she said, with a shrug.

"Recently?"

"Umm—when was the last time?" she wondered aloud.

"Not for a few months," Drumm offered.

"Yes, a few months ago," she said.

"Was there anything on that film that might bear on this investigation?"

"Hardly," she answered. "Why do you ask?"

"No reason," McGuffin replied.

He thanked them and said good-bye, then left and started slowly up the beach. True, there was no reason a home movie should have any bearing on this investigation, but unless he was mistaken, Mark Drumm's ears had pricked up at the mention of it. McGuffin was confused. Maybe I'm getting too old for this business, he said to himself.

15

McGuffin hated Sundays with all the passion of a divorced man. At home they meant artificial time with his daughter, wandering through Golden Gate Park, asking the same dumb questions of last week and receiving the same patient answers. Out of town it was worse. Everything he had set into motion during the week came to a halt, even crime. He stretched breakfast and the Sunday *Times* to their breaking point, then went to Westwood to see the new Ben Volper film, *Lemmings,* hopeful perhaps that it might provide some insight into its producer. It didn't.

Volper's films, largely unsung while he lived, were now being shown in art houses all across town, and critics were writing tomes in the *Times* about the Volper aesthetic. McGuffin couldn't understand any of it. Each film seemed moderately interesting (*Fields of Flesh* by far the best), but there was no continuum running through the work that he could see. Nevertheless, he was glad that the public had finally taken Volper to its heart, if only for his father's sake. Certainly not for Jenny Lang's sake. He thought of Jenny Lang and Mark Drumm, shaking his head sadly, as he wandered aimlessly past the shops and restaurants of Westwood, one of the few places in Los Angeles where people walked. Indeed, it had the look of a place designed solely for walking and shopping, then stamped out of plastic and dropped on the city. Nothing in Los Angeles seemed real to McGuffin. Least of all Jenny Lang.

It was possible that she was telling the truth, that she was lonely and looked to her husband's best friend for comfort. But it was just as possible, McGuffin knew, that she and Mark Drumm had been lovers for some time prior to her husband's death. And it was further possible that they had killed Volper when he became aware of her betrayal and threatened divorce. It was a plausible theory, but it didn't explain why Victor Wenner had disappeared, or why his apartment had been ransacked, or why Mahoud had tried to kill him.

As a matter of fact, McGuffin decided, as he prowled the municipal parking lot for his car, it was a lousy theory that only created more problems than it solved. And besides, he still preferred to give Jenny Lang the benefit of the doubt.

He was beginning to worry that he had lost still another rental car, when suddenly it came into view. McGuffin decided to treat himself to dinner at a posh Beverly Hills eatery where movie stars were known to hang out, an ersatz turn-of-the century saloon where singles gathered at the bar. His suit set off a ripple of interest when he stepped inside, probably because there were no stars this night and little of interest going on. He sat at a table in the back room, ordered a steak, and waited. When it came, he ate slowly and sipped Calistoga water. He thought of calling Erin Green when he had finished dinner, but decided against it when he learned the phones were on the second floor. Instead he paid his bill and made his way slowly back to the Beverly Hills Hotel. He would buy a magazine, or maybe another mystery, read for a while, and turn in early. He had to be keen for his meeting with the district attorney in the morning.

He stopped at the desk before the magazine stand and learned that Erin had apparently had the same idea as he had had earlier. She had phoned him at four and again at six. McGuffin glanced at his watch—it was almost ten—too late for love.

"There's one more," the desk clerk informed McGuffin, as he started for the magazine stand.

It was from David Hochman. It said simply, "Please phone, urgent." The "urgent" had been underlined several times.

"What time did he phone?" McGuffin asked.

"He didn't," the clerk replied. "He came by earlier this evening, but you were out, so he left this message. He seemed rather anxious to see you, Mr. McGuffin."

"Thanks," McGuffin said, as he turned and walked to the magazine stand. He had been right; Hochman was the weak link. He knew something and he didn't want to go the way of Volper and Wenner. He bought the *Atlantic Monthly* for an article on President Reagan and hurried back to his room.

He phoned Hochman immediately, but the line was busy, so he lay on the bed with the magazine and began reading about Ronald Reagan. When the phone rang a few minutes later, McGuffin pounced.

"Hochman?"

"No, it's Goody," a familiar raspy voice replied.

"Goody, where are you?"

"I'm at my joint, where the hell else would I be?"

"I thought you might be in L.A.," McGuffin replied.

"That'll be the day," Goody snorted. "Listen, some guys have been asking about you, I thought you ought to know."

"What guys?"

"Cheap suits, funny hats? Said they were investigating you for a job."

"FBI?" McGuffin asked.

"In spades. I don't know what you're into this time, Amos, but these guys are asking some very funny questions of a lot of people. They been talking to practically everybody who comes in here."

"What sort of questions?" McGuffin asked.

"Political questions. Does he vote? Who does he vote for? How does he feel about the Shah of Iran, the Ayatollah Khomeini? Stuff like that. I told them I didn't think you knew those guys. What are you into, Amos? I thought you were just looking for a missing movie producer."

"That's all I am doing," McGuffin replied. "Maybe they want me to run for office."

"Yeah, commissioner of alcohol. Listen, this is my nickel, if I hear anything more, I'll give you a call."

McGuffin thanked him and hung up, then lay back and stared at the ceiling. What the hell have I done to flush out the FBI? he asked himself. He could think of nothing.

More than half an hour later, he phoned David Hochman for a second time and still the line was busy. When, fifteen minutes later, the line was still busy, McGuffin decided to drive over to Hochman's house and see whom the writer was talking to.

The lights were out at Hochman's house, but the white Rolls-Royce glowed luminously in the drive in front of the door. McGuffin parked at the curb and walked quickly across the lawn to the front door. He rang and waited, then rang again, but got no answer. He tried the door, but it was locked, so again he went to his American Express card. He slipped it between the door and the frame, up against the guard bolt, then worked the bolt back until the door fell quietly open. Removing the automatic from his pocket, he eased the safety forward and slipped inside.

The French doors at the end of the entry hall were open and the moonlight through the trees in the garden lay scattered on the floor like pieces of a shattered mirror. It was pretty, like a movie set, but something was wrong. When he moved down the foyer, past the portraits of past wives and present children, something moved in the garden and McGuffin flattened himself against the wall. Then he saw— it was only one of Hochman's cats. They were sitting, at least half a dozen of them, around the swimming pool, like silent statues.

At the end of the hall he felt along the wall beside the French doors, found a light panel, and turned the top switch. The underwater lights from the swimming pool came on, giving off an eerie blue glow that explained the silent vigil of the cats. David Hochman was floating facedown in his swimming pool.

McGuffin found a rake leaning against the side of the house and with it pulled the body to the stairs at the shallow end of the pool. Hochman's body was fully clothed, in perhaps the same work shirt and jeans McGuffin had first seen him wearing, and his face, he saw, when he rolled the body over, was the same blue-white hue as the light that shined through the water. There was a package of cigarettes in his breast pocket and several butts floating on the water. The kid from the Bronx, who couldn't swim a stroke, had drowned in his ashtray.

When he let the body go, it slid down the stairs, turned, and came to the surface. McGuffin returned the rake to the side of the house and wiped his prints from the handle. It wouldn't do to be found here, or to be the one to find the body—police questions and a coroner's inquest would only hamper his own investigation. He took a quick look around—everything was the same as he had last seen it; the desk with the word processor and basket of movie ideas lay undisturbed under the fringed umbrella, along with the two wireless phones. It was the stuff of cheap detective movies, McGuffin knew, but he wondered if the screenwriter might have left a message on his word processor. Feeling foolish—McGuffin didn't know how to work the machine, nor did he expect to find anything written there—he found the switch and flipped it on. The machine hummed softly as a dull gray screen came to life. This, McGuffin realized, in spite of his woeful ignorance of things electronic, would be the page. It was blank except for two words near the bottom: FADE OUT. So much for cheap hunches, McGuffin said to himself as he switched the computer off.

He turned and started back into the house, then froze. Standing in the hall, just beyond the reach of the moon, stood the figure of a large man, silhouetted for an instant by the light of a passing car in the street beyond the open front door. Becoming unfrozen, McGuffin moved his hand slowly for his jacket pocket.

"Don't even think of it," a familiar, high-pitched voice warned. It was Pedro Chan.

Chan stepped into the moonlight, gun drawn, and walked across the patio to McGuffin. He took the automatic from McGuffin's pocket and, with familiar ease, removed the clip and snapped the loose round out of the chamber.

"You got a permit for this?" he asked, as he slipped the gun into his own pocket.

"At the hotel," McGuffin answered.

"Shame on you. You know you're supposed to have it with you. But then I understand you've been doing a lot of things lately that you're not supposed to be doing," he remarked, as he walked to the edge of the pool.

"I think we both know I didn't kill David Hochman," McGuffin replied.

"Yeah, I think we can agree about that," Chan said, nodding at the floating corpse. "Looks like David Hochman fell into his pool and drowned."

"Or maybe he was pushed."

"If I thought that, I'd have to take you in," he said, turning to face McGuffin. "And I don't think you'd like that."

"I'd like it a whole hell of a lot better than being shot right here."

"I'm gonna give you another choice," Chan said. "I'm gonna give you the chance to get out of town alive. I could put you in a bag and drop you in the pool, but because you're a friend of Frangiapani, I'm gonna give you a break. And you're gonna take it. You're gonna be on a plane for Frisco by noon tomorrow, or your ass is grass. You understand what I'm saying, McGuffin?"

"I understand perfectly," McGuffin said.

Only a moment ago he would have given ten to five that Chan was going to kill him. And now, even though he knew that Chan had killed Hochman (or was all but certain) Chan was letting him go. He must think I'm one scared private eye, McGuffin decided. Okay, if that's what Chan wanted, McGuffin would give it to him.

"And you don't have to worry about a thing," McGuffin assured him. "I didn't see anything and I don't know anything. I'll be on that plane for San Francisco first thing in the morning and you'll never see or hear from me again."

A faint look of disgust crossed Chan's face as he watched and listened to McGuffin. "Get the fuck out of here," he ordered.

"Yes, sir," McGuffin said, backing to the door. Then he remembered. "What about my gun?"

Chan tossed the gun in the air and McGuffin caught it.

"Okay, fine—I'll be there," McGuffin said, stuffing the gun in his pocket while backing down the hall. "First thing in the morning!" he called, then turned and hurried out of the house.

"I'll be there all right," McGuffin muttered aloud, as he started the car. "With the district attorney."

He made an angry U-turn at the corner and sped back to the Beverly Hills Hotel, luxurious refuge from a mad world of cocaine financiers and murderer cops. I may be getting too old for this business, McGuffin allowed. But not too old to bust a crooked cop.

16

Assistant District Attorney Rosen allowed McGuffin to wait for fifteen minutes in Reception before showing him into the large corner conference room where his boss waited with two other men. One of them was Pedro Chan.

"What the hell is going on?" McGuffin demanded, even before the introductions.

"Please, sit down, Mr. McGuffin, the man in charge instructed, pointing to the chair opposite him at the conference table. He was round and pink, with the last precious strands of long sandy hair sticking to his shiny pate like brush bristles on restained oak. Chan and the other man sat on either side of him.

McGuffin sat uneasily. The whole thing had the look of a kangaroo court and, judging from the seating arrangement, he, not Chan, was to be the defendant. Rosen took the chair next to him. Apparently he was to be the court-appointed defense attorney.

"This is Mr. Fitzpatrick, special assistant to the district attorney," Rosen said of the fleshy man opposite McGuffin. McGuffin nodded tersely. "This is Mr. Brown and of course you know Officer Chan."

McGuffin did not acknowledge Chan's nod. "Who's Mr. Brown with?" he demanded.

"Mr. Brown is a federal officer," Fitzpatrick replied.

"Which department?" McGuffin persisted.

Fitzpatrick began to object, but the gray-haired man silenced him with a raised hand.

"The State Department," he replied. He looked to be about sixty, a well-made little man with a white military mustache and neatly trimmed gray hair. CIA, McGuffin guessed. What the hell is going on?

"I understand you've been asking a lot of questions about me in San Francisco," McGuffin challenged.

"And did I learn anything?" Brown asked, with a fake smile.

"Knowing how the CIA works, I doubt it," McGuffin answered. Brown stiffened, then cleared his throat and smiled quickly, a momentary but revealing loss of composure that wouldn't happen again. "You could have learned a lot more from me than you ever could from my friends," McGuffin informed him.

"Shall we get on with this?" Brown asked of Fitzgerald.

"Yes, let's," Fitzgerald said, carefully arranging his hands on the table in front of him.

"Quite frankly, Mr. McGuffin, we hadn't expected you here this morning. Officer Chan was quite convinced that after last night's encounter, you had been persuaded to leave town."

Confused, McGuffin glanced at Chan, who gave him an enigmatic little salute. "He told you about last night—?"

"Let me begin, Mr. McGuffin, by disabusing you of the notion that Officer Chan is a cop gone sour," Fitzgerald said. "In fact, nothing could be further from the truth. Pedro has worked very closely with this office in the last several years— and he is right now—on the Aba Ben Mahoud affair."

"He may be working a little closer than you think," McGuffin interrupted. He turned to Rosen, who sat beside him, pen poised over legal pad. "Did you tell your boss that Chan threatened to kill me?"

Rosen nodded as Chan laughed and slapped the desk. "That was an idle threat, McGuffin! I tried to scare you off the Mahoud case—last night I thought I did—but you're a sneaky bastard, aren't you?" He laughed again.

"It keeps me alive," McGuffin replied. "Now somebody better tell me what's going on. I came here with solid evidence that Chan is sheltering a dope dealer and trying to score a shipment for himself, and you tell me he's a straight cop. He just admitted that he threatened to kill me and you believe him when he says it's only an idle threat. Where am I, in the district attorney's office, or Disneyland?"

"You're in the district attorney's office, all right," Fitzgerald said, with a big pumpkin smile. "And I wish I could tell you a lot more, you deserve it," he said, with a nod toward McGuffin's battered face. "But I can't tell you anything other than the fact that Mahoud is under constant surveillance by this office in the person of Pedro Chan."

"Surveillance or protection?" McGuffin interrupted.

"Surveillance," Fitzgerald insisted, unperturbed by McGuffin's refusal to believe him. "You're right, Mahoud is in the drug business. And when we're able to make a case against him, we'll arrest him. But that's a very tricky proposition. We can't move until we have everything tied down. You're a private investigator, you understand that—and a very good one, Pedro tells me."

"You're all full of shit," McGuffin muttered impatiently.

"Perhaps," Fitzgerald agreed amiably. "Sometimes we succeed, sometimes we screw up. But give us this, Mr. McGuffin, we're doing our absolute best to get Mahoud. And I think we will if we can have your cooperation."

"What kind of cooperation?"

"Stay away from Mahoud. Leave him to us."

McGuffin looked at Fitzgerald, then at Chan. "Leave him to you...And what about Ben Volper and Victor Wenner and David Hochman—the guy you found in the pool last night—and all the other people he's going to kill while you sit around building your case?"

Fitzgerald looked at Chan, shook his head, and made a hissing noise. "You tell him," he said.

Chan sighed and spoke wearily. "Mahoud didn't kill those people. You're gonna find it hard to believe, but we've been watching him for months. We know when he farts, and we know he never went near any of those people."

"What about his spring?"

"His what?"

"Bodyguard, a third party, a hired assassin. Mahoud

doesn't have to do it himself!" McGuffin was becoming impatient with such obstinacy in the face of clear fact. A little more of this bullshit and he'd get up and go directly to the newspapers.

"We know everybody he's in contact with; he has no friends, he's a loner," Chan insisted.

"Sounds to me like a very thorough surveillance for one dope dealer," McGuffin observed.

"It is," Fitzgerald answered. "The biggest we've ever conducted out of this office."

"And still you don't know that Volper and Wenner and Hochman were selling dope for him?"

"We know all about it," Chan answered.

"Then what are you waiting for? Why don't you round them up and start a choir? Or would you rather wait until Mahoud kills them all?"

"Damn it, McGuffin, Mahoud didn't kill anybody!" Chan shot back, becoming angry now. "I told you that, and you're just gonna have to take our word for it."

"I'm not taking the word of anybody here," McGuffin said calmly. "I may not be the smartest private detective on the West Coast, but I've got the best nose—I know bullshit when I smell it and I smell it now. You're protecting Mahoud and it's got something to do with him," McGuffin charged, pointing to the CIA man. "Fine, that's your business. But finding out what happened to Ben Volper is mine. Now this thing may be getting a little too big for me," McGuffin said, with a nod to Mr. Brown, as he prepared to get up from the table, "but I know an estate that can handle it quite nicely."

"What estate?" Fitzgerald demanded, as McGuffin got to his feet.

"The *Fourth* Estate."

"You're not going to the newspapers!" Fitzgerald cried, jumping to his feet.

"Watch me," McGuffin said, as he turned and started for the door.

"Come back here, Mr. McGuffin." It was Brown's voice, calm, used to command.

McGuffin stopped and turned. "Go fuck yourself." Then he turned and continued to the door.

"I'll tell you everything you want to know," Brown promised.

McGuffin released the doorknob, turned, and walked back to the desk. Rosen adjusted his chair and McGuffin slid into it and waited.

Mr. Brown placed his elbows on the table and regarded this troublesome detective with what seemed like bemusement. He wore French cuffs, linked by large Roman coins. The gold glittered against his gray suit, like nuggets in silt. "Pedro said you were a pest," he said.

McGuffin thanked him and waited for the explanation.

"Your nose is good," Brown went on. "We've invested a great deal more in the surveillance of Mr. Mahoud than we ordinarily would for a mere narcotics dealer, and with good reason." He reached under the table and brought out a scarred briefcase. He opened it and removed a large photograph, which he slid across the table to McGuffin. "Is this Mr. Mahoud?" he asked.

McGuffin studied the photograph. It was a younger man with a thick, dark beard and a great pile of curly hair standing before a columned building, but it was unmistakably Aba Ben Mahoud. "Yeah, that's him," McGuffin acknowledged and pushed the photo back across the table.

"At the time that picture was taken, several years ago, he was Professor Mahoud, teaching Persian culture at New York University," Brown informed him, as he fished in his bag for another picture, which he slid across the table to McGuffin. "And this one?"

This one looked more like the present Aba Ben Mahoud, sans beard, with shorter hair, though not so short as now. It showed him at the head of a parade under a banner that read RETURN THE SHAH. "This is him," McGuffin confirmed.

"Shortly after this picture was taken, Mahoud disappeared, following an attempt on his life in Greenwich Village; some say by the Shah's security forces. We honestly don't know if this is true or not; nor does it matter. What matters is this," he said, handing McGuffin a third picture.

This one showed him standing beside a familiar figure.

"That's—" McGuffin couldn't remember the name that had dominated the news such a short time ago.

"Gotzbadeh," Brown supplied. "It was taken during the hostage negotiations. Although Mahoud is a leftist, he quickly became disenchanted with the Ayatollah, and at the time this picture was taken he was our man in place."

"A CIA agent," McGuffin said softly.

"I can neither confirm nor deny," Brown recited, as he returned the photograph and snapped the briefcase closed. "In any event, he's no longer working for us—at least not directly."

McGuffin wasn't paying attention. He was remembering Mahoud's schoolmaster manner and all the foreign publications in his library, certainly more fitting for a college professor than for a dope supplier. Only his violent nature seemed inappropriate.

"He tried to kill me," McGuffin said, interrupting Brown's lecture.

"Of course," Brown answered. "He thought you were working for the Ayatollah."

"Me?" McGuffin asked.

"Aba Ben Mahoud is right at the top of the Ayatollah's hit list. He's a top-ranking officer in the Muhajeddin-i Khalq, the Muslim socialist party dedicated to the overthrow of the Ayatollah. We don't exactly cotton to the kind of government Mahoud has in mind for Iran, but right now he's the only game in town, so we do what we can to help him."

"You mean," McGuffin began slowly, "the federal government is helping Mahoud distribute drugs?"

"I can neither confirm nor deny," Brown repeated. "But I can tell you this—Aba Ben Mahoud is not a drug dealer in the usual sense. The money he makes from drugs is being used to supply arms to the Muhajeddin in Iran. Mahoud is able to do things that our government can't do and it doesn't behoove us to see it stopped."

"Not even if he's killing Americans?"

"Mahoud didn't kill those people," Brown said, stroking his bristly mustache with his fingertips. "In the last two and a half years, Mahoud has done nothing of which we are not aware. If you'd like, I can give you a transcript of your entire conversation with Mahoud in his house."

"Yeah, I'd like to see that," McGuffin said.

Again Brown went into his briefcase and came out with a sheaf of papers, which he pushed across the table to McGuffin. It was accurate, McGuffin saw, as he leafed through it, even the part in the wine cellar.

"You knew they were killing me and you didn't do anything about it?" McGuffin said, thrusting the pages back at him.

"It's a mechanical process, Mr. McGuffin. The belts are only transcribed on the following business day."

"How reassuringly old-fashioned," McGuffin said.

"I am sorry to louse up your investigation like this," the federal agent apologized. "I've been up the garden path a few times myself. But you do see, don't you, that Mahoud had nothing to do with Mr. Volper's death or the others?"

This was true, McGuffin knew, only if Brown was telling the truth. And to get McGuffin out of his hair, Brown would probably kill him almost as readily as he would lie to him.

"Why did you tell me all this?" McGuffin asked. "Wouldn't it be safer to stick me with a poisoned umbrella tip, or whatever you guys are using these days?"

"We thought we'd try this first. Or last," he added, without a smile. He did have a sense of humor. "I'm sure you realize the extremely delicate nature of this information, Mr. McGuffin. We didn't mean to make you a part of this, but you rather forced it upon yourself, so to speak." He opened the briefcase again and came out with a burned, scarred briar and a leather tobacco pouch. It was the sort of pipe an army colonel might smoke. "Naturally I had to take certain precautions before divulging this information to you," he said, plunging the pipe into the pouch.

"That's why you ran the background check on me."

Brown nodded as he tamped the pipe. "Your politics aren't a lot different from Mahoud's apparently. A bit leftish—you disapproved of the Shah, but disliked Khomeini even more—but a good American, whatever that is. What I mean to say,

Mr. McGuffin, is that you must never tell anyone what you've heard here today," he said, putting the bit in his mouth.

"You don't have to worry about that," McGuffin assured him. "I'm only interested in finding out what happened to Ben Volper."

"Ben Volper killed himself," Chan said wearily. "When are you gonna face it? The case is closed."

"Then what happened to Wenner and Hochman?" McGuffin demanded.

"Wenner flew off someplace; he'll show up; and Hochman fell in his swimming pool and drowned. I don't have any trouble with that," he said, palms up, helplessly.

"Well I do," McGuffin muttered.

"It's his nose," Fitzpatrick said, as Brown's pipe lighter flared beside him.

"Umm." Brown nodded, as he sucked sibilantly on his pipe, clouding his face in puffs of blue smoke. Having lighted the pipe, he removed it from his mouth and waved smoke away. "And what if Mahoud did kill these people, Mr. McGuffin? Dope dealers stealing from their supplier? They aren't entirely blameless, are they?"

"You might have to justify murder in your business, but I don't," McGuffin told the agent.

"I thought you were a private investigator, Mr. McGuffin, not a bishop," Brown replied, a note of irritation creeping into his voice. "In Iran people are being killed every day—innocent people, not dope dealers."

"That's not my responsibility," McGuffin replied.

"It is now," Brown said. "Mahoud and his associates are running millions in arms to the Muhajeddin-i Khalq. If we were forced to arrest Mahoud, that flow would stop. Admittedly," he said, waving his smoking pipe in the air, "that would not stop the Muhajeddin—zealots of either stripe are not so easily dissuaded—but it would seriously set them back. Would you like that?"

"Mahoud's end may be honorable," McGuffin agreed. "But that doesn't justify the means."

"What utter nonsense," Brown replied. "I was led to believe that you were a realist, not a Boy Scout."

McGuffin reddened. It was not what he had meant to say. He was fumbling for arguments. He disapproved of drugs as much as he disapproved of Khomeini, but to be forced to choose suddenly between these two evils was too far-fetched and unfair to admit to reason.

"Somehow I can't believe that the future of a country depends upon our allowing one man to continue in the dope trade," McGuffin murmured, burrowing into his wide-shouldered suit.

Brown sighed patiently, as if about to lecture a child. "It might surprise you to know how many unofficial agreements we have with various foreign governments not to prosecute their drug dealers. We knew throughout the Vietnam War that the military high command of South Vietnam was engaged in the drug business, but there was nothing we could do about it, short of dismantling the military apparatus."

"That might not have been a bad idea." McGuffin sulked.

"Perhaps. Bribery is unfortunately as much a part of politics as it is of commerce. Sometimes for good purpose, sometimes for bad. These are case-by-case decisions that we in the State Department are called upon to make every day. Do we want the release of an American tourist who was thrown into a Turkish prison for smuggling a few ounces of cocaine into the country? If so, we have to stop criticizing the premiere's brother-in-law for growing poppies on his country estate. If we want a military base, we have to allow a little more. It's never as simple as your Boy Scout aphorisms, Mr. McGuffin," he said, with ill-concealed disgust for the detective's innocence.

McGuffin's chair squeaked as he sat up straight. He had come expecting to hang a corrupt cop and instead found himself in a Jesuitical exchange with a Jamesian pragmatist. He felt ill-equipped to discuss philosophy, let alone decide the fate of a nation at one sitting.

"What would happen if I were to disclose what I've learned here?" McGuffin asked.

"To you, nothing," Brown answered. "Retribution would only validate your charges. These gentlemen would deny that I was ever here. They would claim that you came here with information that Aba Ben Mahoud was trafficking in drugs and Detective Chan was protecting him. They would say that they investigated and found the charges unwarranted, and that would be the end of it. It would then be up to you to prove your charges, Mr. McGuffin. And if you failed, you would be made to look very foolish, and Mahoud would continue his operation. Could you prove those charges?" Brown asked, as he stuck his pipe in his mouth, confident that no further reply would be necessary.

He was right, McGuffin knew. He had no proof that Mahoud was a drug supplier, gun runner, or murderer. He had only his nose.

"You know I couldn't," McGuffin answered.

Brown removed the pipe from his mouth and smiled. "Then why do anything? Mr. Volper is presumably dead. Is his memory going to be served by proving that he was a drug dealer?"

"No," McGuffin admitted. It was this that McGuffin dreaded telling Nat Volpersky, almost as much as the fact that his son was no longer alive. It was hard enough to punch an old man in the stomach, but to follow up with a right to the jaw was unconscionable. Brown was giving him an easy out; Mahoud was after Khomeini—he had no moral problem there, but the drugs still bothered him.

"The case is closed," Chan put in. "Go back to San Francisco, tell the old man his son was a perfect man in an imperfect world. Let him at least have his memories."

"But—it's a lie," McGuffin said, hesitantly.

"A charitable lie," Fitzgerald pointed out. "The truth is gratuitous cruelty."

"It isn't your ego, is it, old man?" Brown asked, in his clipped, military manner.

"Ego?" McGuffin said.

"You know, being forced to withhold much of what you've learned—play dumb, as it were. That doesn't bother you, does it?"

"No, that doesn't bother me," McGuffin replied. Or does it? he wondered. If it was a kindness to lie to Nat Volpersky, if Ben Volper had been a drug dealer for professional but nevertheless selfish needs, and if Aba Ben Mahoud was a patriot intent only upon overthrowing an oppressive regime, what possible reason could he have for exposing Mahoud? Would Nat feel better because his son's murderer was going unpunished, protected by the State Department and the Los Angeles district attorney's office, for political reasons? Obviously not, he had to admit. Yet something continued to bother him. Was it the drugs and the ugly things they did to people? Or was it simply his pride, the knowledge that he had solved a case to its fullest, and no one would ever know. McGuffin sighed. Maybe this was to be one for his memoirs.

"All right," he said. "The case is closed."

Brown rose and reached across the table for his hand. "Thank you, Mr. McGuffin," he said simply.

Then the others were on their feet, shaking hands and congratulating McGuffin, as if he had just joined an exclusive club. As McGuffin thanked them, he remembered Groucho Marx's words that any club that would have him wouldn't be worth joining.

17

The next day marked the beginning of the winter rains. The western sky was the color of bruised plums, except for the lightning that flashed occasionally beyond the horizon of the sea, like artillery at a distant front. It was more like machine-gun fire when it finally came, spitting at the dry, fire-ravaged hills, probing bullet-nosed drops into ever widening cracks, and collecting and expanding until great chunks of hillside lost their grip and fell into formerly dry arroyos, now awash in swirling, clay-stained water, grasping relentlessly at bridges and cars and sandbagged houses.

McGuffin marveled at how quickly it had come, from an early warning on the television news, to an amorphous gray veil at noon, and now. as he proceeded along the highway to Malibu, slanting gray daggers that drummed in staggered gusts of wind that whipped the tiny car from the side of the road to the white line and back again, as if it were a flag. Only the thought of better weather beyond Santa Barbara kept him going.

He would drive leisurely along the coastal route—he hadn't done it in several years—look for migrating whales, have lunch at Nepenthe, and arrive at Goody's in time for his first drink in more than a week. Then on the following day he would phone Nat Volpersky with the bad news, but not all of it. The cinema history books would record that Ben Volper was a suicide, the victim of a crass Hollywood system that denies the artist the right to express himself. It was similar to the way McGuffin felt, knowing what he did about Aba Ben Mahoud, but being unable to express it.

Today's *Times,* on the car seat beside him, was carefully folded over to the small item on David Hochman's death. "Writer Drowns in Own Pool" was the headline. Little was made of the accident itself—it was a common cause of death in Southern California, like freeway accidents and cancer— or of Hochman's career in Hollywood. *Fields of Flesh* was of course mentioned, but very little else. His few New York plays and awards were given the most space, despite the fact that he had been living and working in Hollywood for most of his adult life. It was clear in retrospect that David Hochman's professional life had ended on the day he left New York, and all the money in Hollywood couldn't compensate for that loss.

McGuffin had phoned Erin Green to tell her that he was closing the case and to find out if she had heard from Victor. She said she hadn't heard from Vic and she was sorry McGuffin was going. If he ever got back to L.A. he would give her a call, he promised. And she promised that she would call him if she ever got to San Francisco. Each knew the other was lying.

He had also phoned Jenny Lang, but the phone was busy. It seemed that people in Los Angeles spent most of their time driving and talking on the phone. He told himself, as he clutched the wheel to hold the car against the driving wind and rain, that another busy signal wasn't ominous. She had probably just left the phone off the hook so she could fuck Mark Drumm. McGuffin was able to understand her need for a man even so soon after her husband's death. After all, celibacy wasn't going to bring Ben back. What he couldn't excuse was her choice of partners. And I'm not jealous, McGuffin told himself, holding the shuddering car against a sudden gust of wind from the sea. It's not easy to like a guy who tried to blow a hole in your chest. One day that temper is going to get him in big trouble, McGuffin was sure. He would mention this in his final report to Nat Volpersky and send Jenny Lang a copy, he decided, as he approached the Malibu town limits.

The police were directing traffic around a fallen telephone pole, slowing traffic to a crawl. Behind the beach houses, hooded waves were snapping against the seawalls like foamy whips. Waiting in traffic, he began to worry about Jenny Lang's busy phone. By the time he reached the Colony, he was sufficiently worried to stop by her house to see if everything was in order.

There was no trouble getting through the gate this time—trucks filled with sand were grinding through in low gear, defying molestation by the guard huddled in his dry shack. McGuffin slipped in tightly between mud flaps and a silver bulldog and followed the lead truck into the compound. When the truck stopped at an angle in the narrow street, McGuffin was unable to get by. But that wasn't necessary, he saw, when Jenny Lang, in a yellow slicker, pushed through the gate, followed by Mark Drumm, pushing a wheelbarrow, and Isaac Stein and Judy Sloan, both carrying shovels. It was the entire Bronx Social Club, minus its two recently deceased members, turned out in slickers to sandbag the clubhouse.

They stood at the side of the truck, backs to McGuffin, as the truck bed rose in the air. The wet sand held for a moment, then collapsed and fell to the street. With the bed still lifted, the driver pulled forward a few feet to allow the last of the sand to fall from the truck, then lowered the bed. When the empty truck moved off, the Bronx Social Club went to work. Stein and Sloan filled the wheelbarrow and Drumm pushed it through the gate, followed by the other three. There seemed to be nothing he could do for Jenny Lang, McGuffin decided. Mark Drumm was taking care of everything. Then the sky opened and rain fell like sand from a truck, all but concealing the house a scant twenty yards away. He turned the car around and drove carefully toward the highway in the blinding rain. He would be glad to see San Francisco.

18

It was after midnight when McGuffin finally arrived in San Francisco, exhausted by the storms that had followed him most of the way up the coast. He drove directly to Gino's gas station, parked the car, and limped stiffly across the Embarcadero to the *Oakland Queen*. He was too tired even for a nightcap at Goody's.

He walked up the gangplank and onto the boat, opened the front door, and walked down the gleaming passageway between two rows of glass-walled offices. He climbed the spiral stairs at the end of the boat, opened the door to the wheelhouse, and stepped inside. There were several pieces of mail and a note from Elmo on the floor, he saw, when he switched on the light and closed the door. He threw the mail on the bed and read Elmo's note.

> While you were gone, someone stole all the potted palms from the front deck. See me immediately!!!
>
> Elmo

McGuffin crumpled the note and threw it in the wastebasket. He thought something had looked different the moment he had stepped aboard the boat. There would be trouble with Elmo, but he was too tired to worry about it now, he decided, as he began to undress. He dropped his clothes in a pile on the floor and climbed into bed, then lay on his back and listened to the foghorns on the bay. It was the last thing he remembered before the phone rang.

"Mr. McGuffin?"

It was Mrs. Begelman. McGuffin had forgotten that he
was back on service. "Hello, Mrs. Begelman," he mumbled.

"So how was lotus land?" she asked. "I didn't wake you,
did I? It's almost noon."

"No, you didn't wake me." He yawned.

"I'm sorry I woke you. Listen, Mr. Volpersky's been trying
to reach you. He heard you checked out from the hotel—
some hotel by the way, the Beverly Hills yet—and he's
terribly worried. I told him not to worry, there are no planes
getting out because of the storm—what did you do, walk?"

"Drove."

"That's what I told him. Anyway, he's such a nice man—
a widower, by the way. You wouldn't happen to have his
picture?"

"No, I don't. I have his son's picture."

"You can't tell anything from that," she said. "I know so
many beautiful parents, their kids are dogs; you wouldn't
believe."

"What did Mr. Volpersky want?" McGuffin interrupted.

"How would I know? I just take the messages. He wants
you to call. Naturally it's about his son; he's worried sick.
And no wonder. That boy did not commit suicide, Mr.
McGuffin. Not a boy like that who calls his father two, three
times a week, uh-uh, I'm sorry."

"Is that all?" he interrupted again.

"No that's not all. You also got a call from a girl in Los
Angeles named Erin Green. Who's she, somebody you met
down there?"

"Yeah, somebody I met down there," McGuffin said, writing her name beside Volpersky's.

"That's very nice for you. How's your wife?"

"Ex-wife," McGuffin corrected.

"Wife, ex-wife, what's the difference?"

"Do you have anything else, Mrs. Begelman?"

"Only somebody named Elmo who wants you to call him
right away about some missing trees. I told him you were
very busy looking for a missing movie producer and I didn't
think you'd have time to go looking for any farshtinkener

trees, and do you know, Mr. McGuffin, he got very huffy."

"Never mind, Mrs. Begelman. If he calls again, tell him I'm still in Los Angeles, but I'll call him as soon as I get back."

"Things are that tough, you have to take a missing-tree case?" she asked.

"Have a nice day, Mrs. Begelman."

"You too, Mr. McGuffin. And I'm sorry about that crack about the girl in Los Angeles. You're young; God knows, you should have your fun while you can."

"Thank you."

"You're welcome," she said and hung up.

McGuffin dropped the phone in its cradle and swung his feet to the deck. There's something to be said for not drinking, he decided, as he walked painlessly to the bathroom. When he had showered and dressed, he phoned Erin in Los Angeles, but got only her answering machine. "Hi, this is the Erin Green Studio," her message began—no mention of Victor Wenner. He left Goody's number on her machine, then hung up and quickly dialed Nat Volpersky in New York. Might as well get it over with, McGuffin decided.

Halfway through the numbers, McGuffin had a change of heart. He replaced the receiver and inserted a sheet of stationery in the typewriter. "Dear Mr. Volpersky," the report began. "Having concluded my investigation of the disappearance of your son, Benjamin Volper, it is my sad duty to inform you..."

Feeling depressed, McGuffin wandered circuitously to Tadich's restaurant in the financial district. It was a solid old establishment, favored by the locals and avoided by the tourists, a place where he might find a friendly face to cheer him up.

Judge Brennan was there, a napkin tucked in his shirt, presiding magisterially over the large table in the corner. There were a couple of other judges in attendance, a recently retired congressman newly returned to law practice, and his associate, an uncannily successful trial lawyer. Brennan hailed him, and McGuffin brushed by the table, hoping a bit of work might stick to him. The lawyer thought he might have something and promised to call in the morning. McGuffin thanked him and moved on to his table. He ordered a sirloin, medium rare, and a bottle of Carey Cellars, his favorite California wine. He hoped it would cheer him up.

It didn't. A couple of drinks at Goody's might do the trick, he decided. He paid his bill and left, hailed a passing cab on California Street, and directed the driver to Goody's. The after-work crowd had long since departed by the time McGuffin arrived, leaving only the hard drinkers and the unhappily married.

"What happened to your face—you get caught in one of those Los Angeles mud slides?" Goody asked, as McGuffin slid onto his usual stool at the end of the bar.

"This was strictly free-fall," McGuffin corrected. "How about a Paddy's and soda?"

"You're off the case?" Goody asked, his hand hovering over the bottle.

"Yeah, I'm off the case," McGuffin answered wearily.

Goody poured McGuffin's drink and placed it on the bar in front of him. He knew from past experience that McGuffin would tell him what had happened when he was ready. Like a West Point Cadet, all square angles, McGuffin raised his glass and knocked it back.

"A thing of beauty," Goody whispered.

"First one in a long time." McGuffin sighed.

Goody retreated to the opposite end of the bar. He knew what was coming.

There followed a great many more drinks until, after a couple of hours, McGuffin was non compos mentis. He sat alone at the end of the bar (no one wanted anything to do with him when he was like this) wrestling the twin demons, failure and whiskey. Once McGuffin's purpose had become clear, Goody stayed away, venturing down the bar only to give him his drink, as one would feed a lion. When the phone rang, McGuffin did not reach for it as he usually did, but instead let Goody walk down and reach across the bar for it.

"It's for you," Goody said, sticking the receiver in McGuffin's face.

"Who is it?" McGuffin asked, backing away from the offered phone.

"Mr. Volpersky," Goody answered.

"I'm not here," McGuffin muttered.

"For Christ's sake, talk to the poor sonofabitch!" Goody whispered fiercely, suddenly at McGuffin's ear.

"What am I gonna tell him?" McGuffin asked. "That his son is dead? He already knows that."

"He's your client, tell him something!" Goody demanded, pounding a broken-knuckled fist on the bar. "Don't just sit there gettin' drunk, goddamnit!"

"I'm not here," McGuffin replied firmly.

"I'm sorry, Mr. Volpersky. I thought he was here, but he's not," Goody spoke into the phone, glaring angrily at McGuffin.

When McGuffin ordered another drink, Goody fairly threw it at him. The regulars watched. McGuffin was on the way to being 86'd and he didn't seem to care—he seemed to want it.

Toward closing time, when only a few drunks were left at the bar, Goody approached McGuffin as one might a leper.

"Amos," he said, lifting McGuffin's arm and mopping the spill that was staining his jacket.

McGuffin blinked. His eyes were like two piss holes in the snow. "Yeah?"

"How much longer are you gonna do this?"

"Don't worry about me, Goody." McGuffin smiled weakly. "I was dry all the time I was on the case, except for a little wine. I can turn it on and turn it off at will—got no problem with the demon rum. Would you get me another one?" he asked, as he lifted his nearly empty glass.

"In a minute," Goody growled. He slapped the damp bar rag on the bar and leaned an elbow beside it. "First I wanna talk to you—while you can still understand a little somethin'. Because if you keep goin' the way you're goin', you're gonna end up a stew bum."

"Hey," McGuffin cautioned, motioning for silence, "that's strong language. I am not an alcoholic, I can quit whenever I want. I just proved that in L.A. Not a drink, Goody. Not one drink in all that time."

"You're kidding yourself, Amos," Goody warned, shaking his head sadly. "What good does it do to quit drinkin' for a week, then come back here and polish off a case of Paddy's? You haven't cut down on your consumption, you've just rearranged your schedule."

"I'm entitled to a little recreation. Now will you get me that drink?"

"Not yet," Goody answered. "Not until you tell me what's buggin' you. You're not drinkin ' like before, Amos, this is different. You're gonna kill yourself."

McGuffin shook his head and replied softly. "I'm not gonna kill myself."

"You sound disappointed. What's the matter, what happened in L.A.?"

"Nothin'," McGuffin said, raking his empty glass across the rough bar. The noise caused Danny the drunk to look up and mutter at the interruption. "Nothin' happened in L.A., not a fuckin' thing. That's the trouble."

"You blew one," Goody said. "So what's the big deal?"

"I didn't blow it!" McGuffin said, disturbing Danny for the second time.

"Shut up, McGuffin, you're drunk!" Danny called.

"Go fuck yourself, Danny," McGuffin called.

"What a couple of beauties." Goody sighed, sweeping McGuffin's glass off the bar. He mixed a light drink for McGuffin and placed it in front of him. McGuffin reached for the drink, but Goody kept it. "You got involved in somethin' big down there, didn't you?"

McGuffin nodded.

"What about those FBI guys—what'd they want?"

"I can't talk about it," McGuffin said and reached again for the drink.

Goody pulled it away and backed up a step, holding the drink just out of McGuffin's reach. "Did Volper commit suicide?"

"That's what I put on my report," McGuffin answered.

"But you think somebody killed him."

McGuffin reached further, but Goody pulled the drink just out of reach. "Yeah, I think somebody killed him."

"Who got killed?" Danny the drunk called.

"Shut up, Danny!" Goody called back. "And the Feds pulled you off?"

"That's it." McGuffin nodded.

"Why?"

"I can't say." McGuffin leaned out over the bar for the drink, but again Goody pulled it away.

"And you say you're not an alcoholic. Look at you, you're ready to dive over the bar for a drink."

McGuffin blinked, as if Goody's words had been thrown at him, then slowly settled back down on the stool. "Keep your lousy drink," he said.

Instead, Goody brought the drink down heavily on the bar. "Here, take it," he said.

McGuffin looked at the drink for a moment, then pushed it aside. "I'll tell you what happened in L.A.," he said.

In a rambling, drunken manner, interrupted from time to time by Goody's questions, McGuffin told his rabbi what had happened. He was careful not to mention Mahoud or his country by name, referring to him simply as the Arab. Goody understood the ground rules and didn't probe. When McGuffin had finished, Goody stroked his chin with a knobby hand and stared at him for a long time.

"From what you're tellin' me, I gotta go along with the Feds," he said finally. "No matter what you do, the Arab's gonna go on sellin' drugs, right?"

McGuffin nodded. "If the cops won't move against him, there's nothin' I can do."

"And you ain't gonna endear yourself to the old man by tellin' him his son was murdered because he held out on his supplier..."

"No, I'm not," McGuffin had to agree.

"So what's your problem?"

McGuffin thought for a moment, then shook his head slowly. He didn't know. "Somethin's just not right," he said.

"Go home, Amos," Goody advised. "Go easy on the sauce for a while. Everything'll work out."

"Yeah, maybe," McGuffin agreed.

"You want this drink now?"

"No," McGuffin answered.

"Good man," Goody said, and threw it into the sink. "Tell me," he said, quickly washing and rinsing the glass, "what's Jenny Lang like in person?"

McGuffin shrugged. "Just like everybody else. Right now she's worried about losing her house."

"The bank?" Goody asked. What banker could foreclose on Jenny Lang?

"The storms. When I left she was piling sandbags in front of her house to keep the ocean from carrying it away."

"Imagine that," Goody said. "A movie star workin' like a sandhog."

"I'm afraid the magic of the cinema may be gone forever for me," McGuffin said, as he slid off the bar stool. "Thanks, Goody. I'll see you later."

"Take care," Goody called, as McGuffin moved carefully down the bar toward the front door.

"Hey, Amos, how 'bout a ride home?" Danny called, as McGuffin brushed past him.

"I'm too drunk to drive," McGuffin said, as he staggered through the door.

"Hell, I would have driven," Danny mumbled.

"Last call!" Goody said.

19

Monday night was football night. And on football nights the crowd was thicker than on any other night at Goody's. Men sat clutching their drinks, staring at the television over the end of the bar as if scanning the skies for random gods. It was an activity that mystified McGuffin, like pornographic movies. What was the pleasure in watching others having all the fun? He gave up on the game at halftime—after ten or twelve drinks the colors began running together any-way—and retreated to his stool under the television, away from Goody's disapproving scowl.

Shortly before the start of the second half the phone rang and Sullivan, the cop, picked it up. (Had the caller waited a few minutes longer, the phone probably would have gone unanswered.)

"If that's my wife, I just left," Danny called, forgetting that he had been divorced for two years.

"Nah, it's for McGuffin," Sullivan said, letting the receiver dangle on the cord and scrape against the wall.

"I don't want to talk to him," McGuffin mumbled into his glass.

"It's not a him, it's a her," Sullivan said, returning to his place at the bar.

Curious, McGuffin slid off his stool and made his way carefully to the phone.

"Hello?" McGuffin questioned.

"Amos, it's Erin Green," she answered.

"How are you, Erin?"

"Wet," she replied.

"Still raining?"

"Pouring—for three days—nothing but floods and mud slides."

"That's good," McGuffin said, thinking of Aba Ben Mahoud's house on the edge of the cliff. "Hope it falls down with him in it."

"Are you a little high?" she asked.

"No, I'm plastered. What about Victor—have you heard anything?"

"Not a word. But I didn't call about him," she added. "I just wanted to tell you that your film is ready."

"Film?"

"Those outtakes, remember? The home movies of the Bronx Social Club?"

"Oh yeah. How'd they turn out?"

"Not very interesting," she said. "It just shows the Bronx Social Club, all except Ben, sitting around his house laughing and talking. The only mildly interesting item is Mark and Jenny—they've got their hands all over each other in some of the frames."

"Yeah, that is interesting," McGuffin agreed. If Jenny Lang had been getting it on with Drumm, that was surely no way to keep it from her husband. Or maybe it was just as she had said—she had been lonely and Drumm was convenient. Anyway, it no longer concerned him. He was off the case—Mark Drumm and Jenny Lang could fuck their heads off as far as he was concerned.

"The other thing that's curious about these outtakes is that somewhere there's a home movie that goes on for almost three hours," Erin continued.

"A three-hour home movie?" McGuffin exclaimed. He had watched a few that had seemed that long. "What are they doing for three hours?"

"Mostly watching a football game, it looks like."

"How can you tell?" McGuffin asked. He didn't remember a television set in the filmstrips he had viewed.

"You can see the game in the mirror. The Los Angeles

team has sheep horns on their helmets, right?" Erin asked. She was not a big fan.

"That's right," McGuffin replied. "The Los Angeles Rams."

"And the other team is all in black—looks like a bunch of Darth Vaders," she said.

"The Chicago Bears?" McGuffin mused.

"Don't ask me. Anyway, they're all sitting around watching the game. They must have had a lot of money bet, because in the first part of the game they look like they're in shock, but toward the end they look happy. But you know there's something else very funny about this film," she added, as if seeing it now for the first time.

"What's that?" McGuffin asked.

"You know how in a home movie everybody mugs for the camera?"

"Yeah?"

"Well not in this one."

"Maybe that's because they're all pros," McGuffin suggested, with little interest. "Listen, this is your nickel—"

"I know, I just wanted to tell you about the film. Do you want me to send it to you?"

"You keep it—as a souvenir," McGuffin said.

"Along with the cat."

"Yeah, along with the cat."

She reminded McGuffin to look her up the next time he was in Los Angeles and he promised he would, knowing it would be a long time before he got back to Los Angeles. Then he said good-bye and returned to the bar as the teams were coming back out onto the field.

"How's the game going?" McGuffin asked Judge Brennan, who was sitting almost under the television, getting a stiff neck.

"Not so good, the Bears are winning," the judge said.

"That's too bad," McGuffin sympathized.

"I don't understand it—they looked terrible against Los Angeles a couple of weeks ago and tonight they're pushing the 49ers all over the field."

"Football is a mystery," McGuffin said. "Can I buy you a drink?"

"Don't mind if I do," the judge said, his usual answer.

McGuffin was about to hail Goody, when he turned to the judge and stopped. "What did you say?"

"Don't mind if I do?"

"Before that. Los Angeles played Chicago a couple of weeks ago?"

"Two weeks ago Sunday."

"You're sure about that?" McGuffin pressed.

"When I lose fifty dollars, I remember it," the judge insisted.

"Then why did Jenny Lang and Mark Drumm tell me Volper hadn't made a home movie in more than three months?" McGuffin asked himself aloud.

"You got me there," the judge answered.

"There's no reason to lie about a thing like that," McGuffin went on. Then he remembered Erin's observation—nobody was mugging for the camera. And Mark and Jenny had their hands all over each other. Could it be they didn't know they were being photographed? Suddenly images began unreeling drunkenly, at high speed in McGuffin's mind as snippets of conversation came and went in a kaleidoscopic movie. No, not a movie, a play! But what play? The stage was in heavy shadows. Something was going on, something very important was taking place, but he couldn't see or hear. Then he remembered and the lights came up, dimly at first, then brighter, until at last things began taking shape.

"Amos, are you all right?" the judge asked, peering closely at McGuffin.

"What?" McGuffin snapped, as the lights went out on the stage.

"I said, are you all right?"

"Yes, everything is fine—just fine!" McGuffin said, climbing down from the stool. "I'll see you later."

"Where are you going?" the judge called.

"To Los Angeles!"

"What about our drink?"

"Sorry." McGuffin called from the door. "I'm back on the case!"

20

The sun glinting off the wing tip gave way to darkening clouds, then to rain, as the aircraft began its descent over the Los Angeles basin. McGuffin's stomach roiled like the wind outside the pressurized cabin when the plane lurched in descending levels to the slick airstrip, bounced once, and whooshed along the concrete before a thick gray swirl of water and wind. He unfastened his seat belt as the airplane taxied to the commuter terminal, then sat back and sighed audibly. Despite the reassuring statistics of the airlines industry, as well as the dangers inherent in his own profession, McGuffin was more than a little afraid of flying. And he enjoyed it least of all when he was hung over.

He had no luggage to collect—he had left the Virgin, with the gun tucked safely up inside, aboard the *Oakland Queen*, confident of a peaceful solution to the Volper case— so he made his way directly to the nearest auto-rental desk.

When McGuffin gave the clerk his name, she shuffled through some papers, found the one she was looking for, and put up her pencil.

"I'm sorry, Mr. McGuffin, I won't be able to let you have a car," she informed him.

"Why not?" McGuffin demanded.

She said nothing, only pushed a typed memo across the counter, which McGuffin read.

Anyone renting a car to one Amos McGuffin of San Francisco will be discharged immediately.

Ronald Worthy, Pres.

"Isn't that just like Ron," McGuffin said, shaking his head. "As if I were the only guy sleeping with his wife. But please don't repeat that," he cautioned, as he started for the Hertz desk.

"Oh, I won't!" the wide-eyed woman replied.

When McGuffin walked past her desk, on the way to his Hertz car, she was huddled with two other women in matching uniforms, all staring at him as he passed. When he smiled and waved, they busied themselves with papers.

He drove to the Beverly Hills Hotel, through a rain that slanted in from the sea, instructed the attendant to keep his car close by, then hurried into the lobby to register. He pushed past a group of conventioneers and their spouses, huddled about their luggage, angry as wet cats, and walked quickly to the desk. He signed the registration and laid a five-dollar bill on the desk beside his flight bag.

"Tell the boy to leave this in my room; I'll be back later," he instructed, then dashed back to his car.

He turned right at the bottom of the hill on Sunset, into the wind-driven rain, and headed for Malibu, though not to Jenny Lang's house this time. That would come later.

The traffic light at the ocean highway had been blown down in the wind and a cop in a black slicker was directing traffic. Ahead of him, phosphorescent whitecaps collected against the dark sky in great rolling breakers that fell on the beach like wrestlers. McGuffin slowly made his way along the beach road, past mud slides and fallen trees, while police cars with flashing lights sped past on either side. A bulldozer was pushing mud back up onto a steep clay road that had washed out and across the highway, leaving several stalled cars in the ditch beside the road, half submerged in clay-yellow water. It would have been safer to take the freeway, McGuffin supposed, but duller. And his business was on the beach, at a motel, somewhere past Malibu. He didn't know which motel it was, or how far past Malibu it would be, but it would be there. It had to be: the nose was working.

Past the Colony, he began looking. He dismissed the first two as being too close to home—too much chance of being recognized—and settled on the Sunset Motel, a bit farther on. It looked like the kind of place where someone could safely hide out for a couple of days, an anonymous two-story with the highway in front and the ocean in back; the sort of place where a man could check in in the morning wearing street clothes, then return from the beach in the afternoon wearing a bathing suit, and not attract any attention.

He parked as near the office as he could, grabbed the thick manila envelope from off the front seat, and dashed through the rain to the front door.

A gray-haired man behind the desk examined him suspiciously before getting up to unlock and open the jalousie door.

"Thanks," McGuffin said, squeezing quickly through the opening door.

"Gittin' kinda wet out there, ain't it?" the old man said, shuffling back to the desk in house slippers.

"Yeah, I was," McGuffin said, shaking water from the envelope.

"Can't be too careful—lotta crime out here on the beach," the old man said, not missing McGuffin's innuendo.

"So I've noticed," McGuffin said.

"I've got one room left, it's fifty-five a night," he said, going for the key on the wall behind him.

"I'm not staying," McGuffin said, reaching into the envelope for a photograph. It was an eight-by-ten glossy, the kind actors and actresses carry around in thin briefcases and thrust shamelessly on anybody even remotely able to give them a job. This, however, was a publicity picture of a producer, Ben Volper.

"Have you ever seen this man?" McGuffin asked, holding the picture in front of the old man.

He looked at it, then at McGuffin. "Who's askin'?"

"McGuffin. I've been retained by this man's father to find him. It's in his interest that I do."

"What about mine?" the old man asked.

"If you have any information about this man, I'm sure Mr. Volpersky will see that you're rewarded."

The old man considered for a moment, then nodded curtly. "I know who he is."

"Who?" McGuffin demanded.

"Name's Volpersky."

"Shit," McGuffin muttered. "That's his father's name."

The old man shrugged. "So?"

"You've never seen this man in your life, have you?" McGuffin sighed.

"Can't say that I have," he replied.

"Does anybody else work here who might have seen him?"

"Just the old lady, but she don't see nothin' I don't see. Don't even see half as much no more," he added.

"Thanks," McGuffin said, as he turned and started for the door.

"Don't I git somethin' fer tellin' the truth?" the old man called.

McGuffin let the door slam on him and dashed through the rain to the car. It was just the wrong motel, that's all, he assured himself as he backed around and pulled out onto the highway. The theory is still sound.

More than two hours later, however, after having canvassed all the motels from there very nearly to Trancas, McGuffin was beginning to have his doubts. He had driven almost ten miles from Ben Volper's house, scarcely an impossible distance at a time when desk-bound jocks routinely broke the twenty-six-mile record of Pheidippides, but farther than necessary. At a point outside Trancas, where the highway turned away from the sea, a crudely lettered sign pointed to the Sea Motel, down a gravel road between a row of eucalyptus trees. McGuffin pulled off and stopped. The motel was not visible from the highway and the gravel road was scarcely inviting in the storm. If I lose another rental car I'm liable to be blacklisted for life, he thought.

"What the hell," he muttered, and nosed the car down between the eucalyptus trees.

Several hundred feet down he came out onto a smooth, sloping hillside that stretched to the sea, where the glistening tile roof of the motel could be seen between the ending cliff and the battered beach. It was a rambling, yellow stucco complex that clung to the beach like a washed-up coral formation. There were no other buildings in sight. McGuffin's breath came quickly—it was exactly the kind of place he would choose if he wished to hide out for a few days.

He parked between an old station wagon and a primer-splotched pickup truck, the only two vehicles in evidence, and made a run for the office. A young man sitting at a typewriter looked up incredulously as McGuffin burst into the dingy office.

"I'll be damned," he said breathlessly.

"What's the matter?" McGuffin asked.

"Oscar Wilde was right," he said. "Art does not imitate life, life imitates art. Listen—listen to this," he said, snatching the page from the typewriter. He stood and read: "Fade in—Hotel on beach. Outside a storm is raging. A black sedan pulls up and a man in a dark suit, average looking, gets out and hurries inside."

He walked across the room and stuck the page in McGuffin's puzzled face.

"I just wrote that—that was as far as I got—and then you walked in! Whataya think? Isn't that incredible!"

"I'm not average looking," McGuffin said, peering at the page.

"Hey, I'm talking movie average, not average average. Don't be insulted, man. You're perfect. You ever acted before?"

"No."

"Too bad. I'm lookin' for an actor. Well first I'm lookin' for a producer, then I'm lookin' for an actor."

"So am I," McGuffin said, taking the now soggy envelope from under his jacket. "Have you ever—"

"I'm a screenwriter," the kid said, dancing back to his

typewriter. He picked up a sheaf of papers and waved them at McGuffin. "The great American screenplay, right here! You don't come in until late in the movie, but you're very crucial to the story. Say, you don't know any producers, do you?"

"I might," McGuffin allowed.

"No kidding! You think you could get a script to him?"

McGuffin shrugged. "Maybe."

"Fantastic! Who is he?"

"Ben Volper." It got no reaction.

The kid considered for a moment, then shook his head. "What's he done?"

"*Fields of Flesh*? With Jenny Lang?"

"Jesus—he must be old," the kid mumbled.

McGuffin held his tongue. "This is his picture," he said, laying it on the counter.

By his expression, McGuffin knew he had seen him before.

"Volper?" the kid repeated.

"Ben Volper. But he would have used another name," McGuffin said, becoming excited now. His nose was working.

"There was a guy here a couple of weeks ago," the kid said slowly. "But his name wasn't Volper."

"I told you, he would have used another name," McGuffin said impatiently, as he followed the kid to the counter.

The kid lifted a wooden box from under the counter and began leafing through the cards. "We don't get many guests here anymore. The old man wants to sell it for condos, so he's lettin' it go to ruin."

"Listen, the name isn't important—do you know the face?" McGuffin pleaded, sticking it under the kid's nose.

The kid moved the box from under the photograph and continued to look. "Here it is!" he said, pulling a card from the box. "Yeah, that was a Sunday," he informed McGuffin, looking at the calendar on the wall. "It was very weird."

"What do you mean?" McGuffin demanded, clutching the counter tightly.

"He checked in and I hardly ever saw him again."

"How long did he stay?"

"Two days."

"You got a credit-card number?"

The kid looked at the card and shook his head. "Paid cash in advance."

"Naturally. What about a license number?"

"I didn't get it," he answered, looking again at the card.

"You're supposed to get it, the law requires it," McGuffin snapped.

"Hey, I told you, we're goin' condo—things are loose around here."

"Shit," McGuffin growled.

"Does that mean you won't show him my script?"

McGuffin ignored him. "Did he sign that card?"

The kid looked. "He printed it." He jumped when McGuffin slammed his fist down on the desk. "S. Fox," the motel clerk added.

McGuffin paced irritably over the worn linoleum. The kid's eyewitness testimony by itself might be enough to convince a jury that Ben Volper was alive after his supposed suicide. But he had seen too many eyewitnesses fall apart under cross-examination to be satisfied with just the word of one aspiring screenwiter. He wanted independent corroborating evidence.

McGuffin stopped pacing. He had a sudden feeling of déjà vu, of the sort that had hit him last night in Goody's— a stage going from dark to light.

"S. Fox?" he said softly.

"S. Fox." The kid nodded.

"S. Fox!" McGuffin shouted.

The kid retreated to the wall as this madman scrabbled in his soggy envelope for a notebook. He found a ball-point pen and pushed them both at the kid.

"Here, put your name and phone number here," McGuffin ordered.

Cautiously, the kid took the pad and pen from McGuffin and wrote his name and number on a blank page.

"The script isn't quite finished yet," he warned, as McGuffin grabbed the pad and pen away from him.

"It's okay, you're already a very important man," McGuffin assured him, dropping the pad and pen into his pocket. "Let me have the card—and try not to get any more fingerprints on it than you already have," he ordered.

Obediently, the kid dropped the card into the envelope McGuffin extended.

"How soon do you think he'll want to see it?" the would-be screenwriter asked, worried now. "I mean, most of it's still in my head, you know."

"Don't worry about it," McGuffin said, as he crossed to the door. "When the time comes, all you have to do is tell your story—somebody else will write it all down."

The screenwriter beamed. He reminded McGuffin a little of David Hochman.

Savoring his success, scarcely aware of the rain hammering at the windshield, McGuffin sped back to the hotel. Nothing could bother him now—neither rain nor wind nor slippery pavement—Ben Volper had not committed suicide! He had a witness! Now all that remained was to determine what had happened to him—and that would require the help of the Bronx Social Club. He had to get to a phone; arrangements had to be made.

Just past Malibu he was pulled over by the California Highway Patrol and given a ticket for "driving too fast for conditions." He accepted it with a smile. Nothing would bother him today.

21

There were already three cars parked in front of Jenny Lang's beach house when McGuffin arrived promptly at nine that night. In the glow of his headlights, rain danced off the roof of Mark Drumm's red Ferrari like a silver halo. The car ahead of that, a dark Porsche, would be Isaac Stein's, and the Mercedes sedan, Judy Sloan's, he supposed. Duly humbled, the detective extinguished the lights and silenced the engine of his rented Plymouth. When he opened the door only a few inches, it was as if he were opening a ship's hatch in a storm at sea. Rain lashed at the first opening and the wail of wind and crashing sea fell on him with palpable force. When he stuck his new umbrella through the cracked door and opened it, it snapped up like Marilyn Monroe's dress.

"Shit!" McGuffin grumbled. Forty-nine ninety-five at the hotel boutique. He released it and it flew off into the night like a kite.

He started for the lighted front door of the house, then stopped and splashed back through the puddles to the three parked cars. He tested the hood of each—they were all cold—then ran for the house. By the time he reached the shelter of the porch roof, his ten-year-old trench coat was wet as a storm jib and already beginning to soak through the shoulders of his new suit. He rang once and Jenny Lang, her hair damp, came to the door in a jogging outfit.

"Come in, you're soaked!" she said, quickly opening and closing the door after him.

"Thanks," McGuffin said, dripping water onto the kitchen floor as he looked around. It was the first he had seen of this end of the house. He was amazed at how small it was. Five million doesn't buy much these days, he thought.

"Let me have your coat," she said, already tugging it from his shoulders. "Oh, your jacket is wet too! Let me have it."

McGuffin protested politely while she removed his damp jacket and put it over a hanger. She hung the jacket in the closet and the trench coat from a hook beside the door among a few others, including a fur-lined raincoat. All of them, he noticed, were still wet.

"I see everybody made it," he said, with a nod to the coats.

"Yes, they're in the living room," she said, taking McGuffin by the elbow. "And I'm afraid they're all as confused as I am by this meeting."

"I'll try to clear it up," he said, as he followed her down the two steps into the living room where the Bronx Social Club—minus two—waited.

Judy Sloan sat on the couch to the right, balancing a drink on her leather pants. Her upswept blond-white hair had come undone in places and her silk blouse was open to show a deep cleavage of almost luminous white skin. A large woman, she seemed to McGuffin to have put on several pounds since the last time he had seen her.

"Hello, detective," she greeted, in a voice that sounded like a load of gravel being dumped.

"Glad you could make it," McGuffin said.

"We were wondering if you could swim," Mark Drumm said. He stood on the second step in front of the sliding-glass door, wearing a V-neck sweater and gold chains over his brown hairy chest.

"Yeah, I can swim," McGuffin replied. Unlike David Hochman, he added to himself.

Isaac Stein stood beside him, hands stuffed in his safari jacket, rocking back and forth in his Topsiders. "I hope this is as important as you said it was, McGuffin," the director said peevishly.

"It is," McGuffin said, as a bolt of lightning flashed over

the beach, briefly illuminating the sandbags piled two or three feet above the deck. The light faded in an instant, leaving McGuffin with an image of a beachhead under fire.

Everyone's shoes were wet, McGuffin noticed. And Judy Sloan had kicked her wet sandals off to the side of the couch. It was the couch of the home movie, with the football-reflecting mirror hanging behind. The television set, which had then probably been in the center of the room, was now pushed back against the projection booth at the far end of the room.

"Can I get you something to drink?" Jenny Lang offered.

"Maybe later," McGuffin answered. Drumm was sucking on a Heineken and there was a drink on the step beside Stein's foot. McGuffin and Jenny Lang were the only ones not drinking.

"A cup of coffee?"

"Maybe a cup of coffee," he agreed.

"I'll have to go and get it," she said, starting for the kitchen. "I gave Dolores the night off."

"Please, don't bother!" McGuffin called after her.

"It's no trouble," she replied from the kitchen.

McGuffin stood awkwardly in the middle of the room, as if he were here to give a speech and just realized that he had left it at home. He looked up when a drop of water fell on his head.

"The goddamned roof leaks," Judy Sloan growled.

"Mine's leaking too," Mark Drumm said. "Why is it that nobody in this town can build a house that doesn't leak?"

"Get me another drink, would you?" she asked, waving her glass in the air.

Mark Drumm scrambled down the steps and carried her glass to the bar.

Jenny returned with McGuffin's coffee. "There's cream and sugar on the bar," she said, handing him the cup.

"Thanks, I take it black."

Jenny sat on the couch beside the agent, while McGuffin stood in the middle of the room and sipped his coffee. A puddle was collecting on the tile floor where he had been standing. When lightning flashed again, McGuffin could see

the large dune, still intact, between the house and the breaking surf.

"Have any of these houses been lost?" McGuffin asked.

"Not so far," Drumm answered, as he walked past
McGuffin with his agent's drink. It was neat.

"Thank you, darling," she said, when he handed it to her.
She placed it on the floor beside her bare foot and fished
in her bag for a red package of cigarettes. "We'll be all right
if the wind doesn't shift," she said.

"We?" McGuffin asked.

"Jenny—I wouldn't want to see her lose her house,"
Judy answered, sticking a long, thin brown cigarette between
her thick red lips. The director was immediately there to
light it.

"No, we wouldn't want to see that," McGuffin agreed.

They all watched as Judy Sloan flared smoke through her
nostrils.

"You said you have information about my husband?" Mrs.
Volper began.

"Yes, I do," McGuffin answered.

"Well—are you gonna tell her?" Drumm asked. He sat
in the Eames chair in front of the window, feet on the ottoman, beer bottle resting on his belt buckle.

McGuffin nodded. "Actually it's only a theory at this
point," he began.

"Ah, shit!" Drumm complained, glancing at his gold Ro-
lex. "You got us out here in a typhoon to listen to a theory?"

"The fact that you all showed up long before nine o'clock
leads me to believe that it's a pretty good theory," McGuffin
said.

Drumm brought the bottle almost to his lips, then stopped.
"You been spying on us?"

McGuffin shook his head. "All of your car motors were
cold when I got here, indicating that you've been here for
some time. Maybe since shortly after you got my call."

"So what?" Drumm replied.

"Let him explain his theory," Isaac Stein said, the calm
voice of reason. He stood on the top step, the toes of his
Topsiders edging over, poised as a bird of prey. "I'd like to

find out what's so curious about arriving early for a meeting—especially one about Ben."

"You're right, there may be nothing curious about it," McGuffin agreed. "And there may be nothing curious about standing out in the rain after you arrive. But it does support my theory."

"He was spying on us!" Drumm exclaimed, snapping up in his chair.

"Your raincoats are still dripping wet," McGuffin said, with a gesture toward the kitchen.

"So? We were checking the house," Drumm said. "Anything wrong with that?"

"Keep quiet," Judy Sloan ordered, flashing her agent's smile, "and let Mr. McGuffin tell us about his theory. Go ahead, dear."

"Thank you," McGuffin said. He walked across the room and placed his cup on the coffee table directly in front of her. "You told me you didn't see Ben at all on the day he supposedly drowned himself, is that right?"

Sloan nodded. "None of us did. Except Jenny, of course," she added, with a nod her way. She squinted one eye almost closed as she raised her cigarette and drew deeply.

McGuffin moved away from the coming smoke and addressed Jenny, who sat stiffly beside her, hands pressed tightly against her thighs. "And you discovered Ben's suicide note shortly after he had gone out for a walk on the beach."

She nodded. "A short while later—sometime after ten."

"After all of the Bronx Social Club had arrived—"

"Yes."

"Then what happened?"

"We read the note—we thought it was a joke—but nevertheless we went out to look for him," she said, lifting her hands and pursing her lips, a European gesture of puzzlement that McGuffin remembered seeing in her movies.

"And you found his clothes."

"Yes."

"Just like in the movies," McGuffin said, as he straightened up and turned to the director. "You know that scene, don't you, Mr. Stein—where the hero takes off his clothes, carefully folds them, and leaves them in a neat pile, then walks slowly into the sea? Usually the sun is setting," McGuffin added. "You know that scene, don't you?"

"I know it very well." Stein nodded.

"But in real life it's never done that way. In real life, suicide victims just jump into the water with their clothes on. After all, who wants to wash up on the beach naked and have a lot of strangers staring at him?" McGuffin shook his head and paced in half circles. "I never did understand that scene. I always wonder—what's he doing, saving the clothes for the next of kin? Or," he asked, approaching Stein, "is it just something you directors do for dramatic effect?"

"I couldn't tell you," Stein answered, standing very nearly as still as a wooden Indian on his perch, two steps above McGuffin, against a backdrop of slashing rain and crashing sea. "I've never directed that scene."

McGuffin stood looking up at him, idly stroking his chin. "But if you had, is that the way you would have directed it?"

"Film producers don't take direction," he said. "They just do whatever they like."

"I see." McGuffin nodded, then turned and moved away from the director. "And Ben Volper was a movie person. He learned how a man behaves in a difficult situation by watching his celluloid heroes on Saturday mornings at the Bijou."

"Loews," Stein corrected.

"So if Volper were to stage his own suicide, it's likely that he'd do it just the way he learned in the movies," McGuffin went on over the interruption.

"That's absurd!" Judy Sloan protested, in a voice like thunder. "I've already told you—if Ben's suicide was just a publicity hoax, I would have known about it. I'm his agent! And besides that, I think your theory is all wet. I think Ben took off his clothes just so he could swim through the surf. Ben's not a powerful swimmer and the waves were high that day. Talk about embarrassment at being found naked— how would it feel to set out to drown yourself, then have to come home because you couldn't get through the surf?"

"Umm—I hadn't thought about that," McGuffin admitted.

"Well maybe you should have," she replied, lifting her glass.

McGuffin stood silent in the middle of the room, hand hooked over the back of his neck, staring impassively at the wet tile. He could almost hear and feel their collective sigh of relief at his apparent confusion. He had run his theory up a blind alley; he knew nothing after all. It was this almost palpable feeling of relief—the nose was working—that finally satisfied him that even the most speculative and horrible part of his theory was true.

"But if he knew he'd have to strip to get through the surf," McGuffin began slowly, "why didn't he simply leave the house in his bathing suit?"

"Because that would have alerted me," his widow answered uncertainly.

"Wearing a bathing suit to the beach would have indicated to you that he was contemplating suicide?" McGuffin asked, incredulous. "Wasn't it more curious when he wore his street clothes to the beach?"

"Well—he—he often wore his street clothes to the beach," she fumbled.

"Really?" he asked.

"Look, McGuffin, if you know where Ben is, why don't you tell us and stop with the fucking theorizing already, okay?" Drumm demanded.

"That's another problem," McGuffin said, turning to the actor, who was sitting in the Eames chair with his legs up, clutching his bottle. "If Volper drowned, why hasn't the body been found by now?"

"It's a big fucking ocean, man; there are sharks as big as this house out there. Pardon me, Jenny," he quickly added.

McGuffin shook his head. "It wasn't the sharks that got Ben Volper. At least not the fish kind. He left here wearing a bathing suit under his clothes, walked up the beach, took them off and left them in a pile. Nothing unusual about that. Then he jogged several miles up the beach to a motel he

had checked into earlier that morning. He waited there while
the police searched for him that morning and during the
afternoon, while all of you sat here on this couch watching
a football game."

"Football?" Mrs. Volper asked, over the stunned silence
of the others.

"You probably didn't notice," McGuffin said. "You were
preoccupied with Mark Drumm most of the time."

"I told you there was nothing between us!" Drumm
shouted, springing out of the chair and across the room.

"Mark!" Isaac Stein shouted.

McGuffin set himself to duck a blow, but Drumm held
up at the command from the director.

"Let him finish," Stein said calmly. "Then you can have
your turn."

Drumm shrank a few inches when he exhaled and backed
away.

"Get me another drink," Judy Sloan ordered, in a deep,
even voice.

Obediently, Drumm changed direction and crossed to the
bar.

"I take it you can prove Ben was at this motel," Stein
said. "You have a witness?"

"I have his motel registration—out in the car."

"Signed by Ben?"

"Printed. He registered under the name S. Fox."

"That's ridiculous!" Jenny Lang exclaimed. "I've never
known Ben to use a pseudonym—much less a silly one like
S. Fox. He has more imagination than that."

"Oh, he had a great deal of imagination," McGuffin agreed.
"As well as a sense of humor. That's the reason he chose
the name S. Fox. The S stand for Sly. It was the name of a
play that appeared on Broadway a few years ago—I looked
it up. It also appeared in London in the early seventeenth
century, when it was called *Volpone*. It was written by Ben
Jonson, as I'm sure you all know."

"What the fuck's a play got to do with anything?" Drumm
demanded, from his position behind the bar.

"You should read it," McGuffin suggested. "It's a horrifying play about human greed—but also very funny. Would you like me to tell you about it?"

"No," Drumm replied.

"Go ahead," the director corrected.

"Well, it's about a man, Volpone, who pretends to be dying in order to trick his friends into giving him expensive gifts. At the bedside they pretend to love him dearly so they'll be remembered in the will. But after he's apparently died, they begin voicing their true feelings, which Volpone of course overhears. Sound familiar?" McGuffin asked, smiling brightly at his stunned audience. "Rather like Oscar Wilde said, isn't it? Art doesn't imitate life, life imitates art. Or something like that. Feel free to correct me if my literary references are wrong. I'm a detective, not an artist like yourselves."

"We're all aware of the play," Stein informed him. "It's the analogy to Ben that we find farfetched."

"Do you?" McGuffin said. "It seemed to me you were all anxious to have me believe that Ben committed suicide because he was paranoid. Ben thought everybody was using him, that nobody liked him for himself—except you, of course, his friends from the old neighborhood, the Bronx Social Club. And his wife, naturally," he added, with a nod to Jenny Lang.

She sat on the edge of the couch, shoulders hunched and knees pressed tightly together, listening to the detective's farfetched theory. Judy Sloan sat beside her, sucking furiously on her long brown cigarette, while she waited for her drink. She picked her empty glass up once, looked at it, and replaced it on the coffee table, hoping perhaps that it might have magically filled itself while Mark Drumm was fumbling at the bar. He seemed to have forgotten what he was sent for, as he stood motionless, staring at McGuffin. Only Isaac Stein, standing quietly on the top step, backlighted by an occasional burst of lightning, seemed reasonably calm. McGuffin paced slowly about the middle of the room while they waited for his next word. For the first time he had an inkling of the power an actor onstage must feel when everything is going right. It was a bit heady.

"But Ben was a real paranoid," McGuffin went on. "He began to worry about even his closest friends. So he devised a little test, not unlike Volpone's. He faked suicide."

"That's ridiculous," Judy Sloan scoffed.

"Bullshit," Drumm added.

"Absurd," Stein said.

Jenny Lang said nothing.

Unfazed, McGuffin went on, pacing and theorizing. "He might have done it to get a little free publicity for his new movie too, I don't know. But most important, he wanted to be a spectator at his own funeral. And that's where Victor Wenner came in. He slipped Vic into that projection booth"—McGuffin pointed—"with a sound camera, to film the reaction of his five closest friends to the news of his death."

"How could he do that without my knowing?" Jenny Lang scoffed.

"That was no problem," McGuffin answered easily. "All your husband had to do was distract you in another part of the house for a few moments while Victor slipped in from the deck. The gatekeeper didn't phone because he came by way of the beach, the same way I did, until tonight."

"Are you still theorizing, Mr. McGuffin?" Stein asked. "Or can you prove this?"

"I've seen the film," McGuffin answered.

Finally, Isaac Stein's composure was disturbed. It was a lie, McGuffin knew, but he had seen the outtakes and that had to count for something. More important, from the stunned silence that greeted this lie, McGuffin now knew for sure that the home movie existed and that they had seen it.

"It was the film that threw me off," McGuffin said. "I thought it was Aba Ben Mahoud who had busted up Victor's apartment looking for a bag of coke, and I thought it was Mahoud who had killed him." McGuffin turned to Drumm, who was staring fixedly at McGuffin from behind the bar. The actor had forgotten entirely about Judy Sloan's drink and so had she. "You must have thought I was the world's dumbest detective when I warned you to be careful of Mahoud." Drumm said nothing. "And you did a good job of convincing me that I was on to something, too. You're not so dumb for an actor."

"I'm beginning to think you're very stupid, McGuffin. Even for a detective," Drumm replied, his voice charged with menace.

Ignoring the threat, McGuffin went on. "When Victor got finished that Sunday afternoon, he had a home movie that lasted nearly three hours—not much action, but the kind of dialogue they don't write anymore. Victor developed the film and brought it to Ben's motel room the next day. He warned Ben that he wouldn't like what he was about to see, but Ben watched it anyway. And God knows, he didn't like what he saw. He was devastated by it. He learned that his wife was having an affair with his best friend and that all his friends despised him for his success—a success for which they all claimed credit. After all, it was David Hochman who had written *Fields of Flesh*, Isaac Stein had directed it, Mark Drumm and Jenny Lang had starred in it, and Judy Sloan had put the deal together. I think Ben Volper must have died then, killed by the betrayal of his wife and friends. The rest was just a formality."

Jenny Lang began crying softly, while Judy Sloan, almost invisible with paleness, sat stock-still, her cigarette about to burn her fingers. When it did, she let it fall to the floor and smolder.

"So, after Ben had viewed this horrible film, he called you all together at his house that night. He told you not to tell anyone that he was still alive, I suppose, and none of you did. If you had, things might have been different. As it turned out, you sat watching and listening to yourselves, wishing that you had never been born. Apology was pointless; you had destroyed the man. All that remained was for him to throw you out of his house, his wife too, cut you all off forever. Which he did. I'm a little weak at this point, you'll have to correct me. But I would guess that he told you, Jenny, that he was going to divorce you for adultery—he had your admission on film—and cut you off without a penny. Am I right?"

Jenny sobbed and sniffed and said nothing, but McGuffin

knew he was right. "And as for your lover," he said, with a nod toward the actor, "one way or another, Ben Volper would see that you never worked in Hollywood again. If the scandal of sleeping with your best friend's wife wasn't sufficient to end your career, he'd personally see that you were blackballed with every major studio and independent producer in this town. And those of you who were involved in the cocaine business with Ben might also lose a very nice little second income. The others might not lose much more than an old friend, but you and Jenny were about to lose everything, and that made you a little crazy, didn't it, Drumm? And everybody here knows what you're capable of when you get a little crazy. I know I do," McGuffin said, rubbing the still tender spot on his head where Drumm had hit him with the bottle.

Drumm glared silently at McGuffin, plainly ready to do far worse, as Isaac Stein walked down the stairs to McGuffin's level and stared curiously at him for a moment.

"How am I doing so far?" McGuffin asked the director.

"I'm amazed," Stein answered. "You seem to know everything except the location of the body."

"Bodies," McGuffin corrected, showing two fingers. "Ben Volper and Victor Wenner are buried under the deck."

There was an audible gasp from Jenny Lang.

"Amazing," Stein repeated. "One would almost think you had been there."

"I was here the day the storm began," McGuffin answered. "I saw the four of you building that seawall outside. I didn't see anything strange about it at the time, but later I remembered what Jenny had told me on the first day I was here. Do you remember, Mrs. Volper? You told me that your house was safe from storms, that it was built farther back than the others and had a large dune in front to stop the sea. But when you have two bodies buried under the deck, you can't afford even the remotest chance that the tide might somehow come in and wash the bodies out, can you? That's when I realized why you were all out in the rain desperately filling sandbags and piling them up in front of the deck."

"You're uncanny," Stein said, with what seemed to be genuine admiration. If McGuffin's disclosures disturbed him, he certainly gave no indication.

"Now why don't you fill me in as to what happened after Ben showed you the movie?" McGuffin asked.

"Don't tell him a fucking thing," Judy Sloan croaked hoarsely.

Stein turned to her and shrugged easily. "Why not? He already knows more than enough."

"Far more," Drumm added.

"You're right," Stein began. "Ben threw us all out that night, including Jenny. As you know from the film, the five of us began making big plans when we thought Ben was dead. Mark and Jenny were free to marry. Ben's money and his production company now belonged to Jenny. She would produce David's scripts, I would direct them, Mark would star, and Judy would get ten percent of everything. It was going to be perfect. And then Ben had the bad taste to show up with that dreadful film. The man was insane, paranoia isn't the half of it. However, let's not damn the dead. We were devastated; Ben was going to destroy us. All of our plans would go for nothing, unless we could think of a way to stop Ben."

"And the only way to do that was to kill him."

Stein nodded. "I'm afraid so."

"Whose idea was it?" McGuffin asked.

"Mark's," Stein replied.

"You sonofabitch!" Drumm cried.

"Relax, Mark," Stein said, raising one hand, as a lion tamer might calm an angry beast. "We're all in this together. You must admit, however, that none of us could have done it without you. Mark agreed to do it if the rest of us would go along with him," Stein informed McGuffin.

"That's what I figured," McGuffin said, turning to Drumm. "Just out of curiosity, did you squeeze the trigger when you had my gun pointed at me?"

"As hard as I could," Drumm answered.

McGuffin shook his head. Jenny Lang had probably saved

his life. It would hurt to see her arrested, but he was going to take a lot of pleasure in putting Mark Drumm away for a long time.

"What about Hochman?" McGuffin asked. "Did he agree to go along with your plan?"

"Hochman resisted at first," Stein answered. "He was the weak sister all along—but we eventually persuaded him to go along with the rest of us."

"And that was why you later killed Hochman?" McGuffin interrupted. "He got cold feet and threatened to go to the police?"

"Exactly." Stein nodded. "Poor David was a writer—everything had to have a beginning, a middle, and an end. He saw the end coming—so to speak."

"Yeah, he saw it all right," McGuffin agreed. "I got a call on the night he drowned. He was probably beginning to suspect that you were going to kill him, and he wanted me to protect him until he could get to the cops."

"No doubt," Stein agreed. "The night we dropped in on him—he knew why we had come. We were prepared to kill him the same way we had killed Ben and Victor, but he ran into the garden. Mark tackled him on the grass and we started to drag him back into the house. Then I suddenly remembered that David couldn't swim, so we pushed him into the swimming pool. But you know, he suddenly learned how to swim," Stein said, still puzzled by this. "Or at least how to tread water in a clumsy sort of way. He made it to the side several times. We had to keep stepping on his fingers and pushing him back out into the deep water, until he finally went under."

"Charming," McGuffin said. "And how did you kill Ben Volper?"

"We snuck back into the house after he was asleep," Stein answered. "Mark went into the kitchen for a knife, then we all followed him into Ben's bedroom. Mark stabbed him first. Then we took turns sticking the knife into him, just like *Murder on the Orient Express*. You know the movie?"

"I read the book," McGuffin said.

Jenny Lang was sobbing loudly now.

"Being the director, I naturally got final cut," Isaac Stein said with a quick smile.

"Was Ben still alive after you first—" McGuffin began, as he turned to the bar.

Drumm was gone! He could be in one of the bedrooms, or in the kitchen, McGuffin realized. Isaac Stein stood between him and the sliding-glass door, which was probably locked anyway. Stay cool, McGuffin told himself. He walked casually away from Stein, hands in his pockets, then stopped and turned.

"So after you stabbed him to death, you buried him under the deck—"

"That's right," Stein replied.

"Along with the film?"

"We burned the film. Or at least we thought we had. Ben didn't tell us anything about Victor Wenner—we assumed Ben had shot the film himself. When Ben failed to show up, Victor knew that we had killed him and he decided to set himself up in the blackmail business. He said he had another copy of the film and unless we took care of him, he was going to take it to the police."

"What did he mean by 'take care of him'?" McGuffin asked.

"He wanted to join our company—as a director."

"But you couldn't have that—"

"Not unless it was absolutely necessary."

"So you killed him."

"Mark did. He was beginning to develop a taste for it."

On cue, Mark walked into the room from the kitchen, one hand held behind his back. He stopped at the bar, rested the other hand against it, and smiled at McGuffin.

"And it was Mark who called Erin Green, pretending to be a cop."

"Hello, this is Sergeant Callahan," Drumm said in a high voice, auditioning a piece of his cop impersonation for McGuffin.

McGuffin didn't like it, but it had been good enough to convince Erin Green.

"After we buried Victor, we ditched his car at the airport; it seemed a nice anonymous place. But Victor hadn't given up the film. He kept insisting he didn't have it, so we had to get into his studio and have a look. We didn't want to kill his girl friend—we knew she didn't know anything about the blackmail scheme or the film—Vic was keeping that all to himself. He told us he was getting ready to dump her. So we got her out of the studio and tore the place inside out, but we never did find the film."

"I'm not surprised," McGuffin said. "There is no other film."

"Bullshit," Mark Drumm said.

"What about the one you saw?" Stein asked.

"I saw a few outtakes, that was all."

"He's lying," Drumm said.

"I sincerely hope you are," Stein said. "Because that's all you have to trade for your life."

As he was speaking, McGuffin caught Drumm in the corner of his eye, moving slowly toward him. When McGuffin turned, the actor removed his arm from behind his back, revealing a butcher knife bigger than the sword he had wielded in *The Captain from Tortuga*. At the same time, Judy Sloan, perhaps inspired by the thought of more action, shook herself from her torpor and dashed into the kitchen to get a knife and join the fray. McGuffin backed away toward Isaac Stein, then away from what he saw. Stein was holding an ice pick, which he had apparently been carrying under his bush jacket all the time.

"Wait a minute," McGuffin pleaded, moving toward the projection booth at the end of the room. "Don't you want to hear about how I solved this case?"

"No," Stein answered, advancing with the ice pick ahead of him.

"I'm talking about the keystone," McGuffin said, continuing to move away. Stein was closing in from the left, Drumm from the right, and now Judy Sloan appeared in the middle with a meat cleaver—barefoot, hair astray, looking like a mad witch. The three of them bore down on McGuffin while Jenny Lang, still the reigning sex goddess of millions of middle-aged American men, sat watching from the couch.

"It has to do with the date of the Rams-Bears game!" he babbled quickly. "You told me Ben hadn't made a home movie in three months, but I could see the game in the mirror that had taken place on the day he disappeared! Do you know what I'm talking about?"

"No," Drumm answered, raising the butcher knife high over his head.

McGuffin was almost up against the projection booth when he shouted: "Pedro! Goddamnit, Pedro, get in here!" Nothing happened. McGuffin shouted again as Drumm brought the knife down. McGuffin ducked almost to the floor and dived at Judy Sloan's white feet, bringing her and the meat cleaver to the tile floor, as the butcher knife glanced off the wall behind him. As McGuffin scrambled to his feet, with Stein in pursuit, Jenny Lang pointed to the deck and screamed. Lightning flashed in the sky, illuminating a soggy Oriental giant struggling at the glass door. McGuffin was hit from behind and spilled on the wet tiles. He rolled over and reached for an arm with an ice pick at the end of it. He held the arm as the faces of Mark Drumm and Judy Sloan appeared above him and Jenny Lang continued to scream. Then a great explosion filled the room, followed by shattering glass and the squeaky voice of Pedro Chan.

"Police! Drop it, motherfucker, or I drop you!"

The cleaver and the butcher knife fell to the tile with a heavy clink, as McGuffin felt the wrist in his hands go limp. Pedro bounded across the room, graceful as a grizzly, kicked the knives across the floor, and pulled Stein off McGuffin as if he were nothing but a rag doll.

"Jesus," McGuffin complained, getting to his feet. "You sure took your fucking time!"

"I couldn't get the fuckin' door open," Chan explained, slamming Stein against the projection booth. "Splay 'em!" Drumm was next. Judy Sloan went to the wall without any help, while Jenny Lang remained on the couch, sobbing hysterically. "Get on the phone and get some cops out here!" he ordered, before McGuffin could protest.

"You can't get the door open—and you didn't bring any

cops with you?" McGuffin exclaimed. "You coulda got me killed!"

"You're lucky I'm here at all," Chan said, snapping handcuffs on Stein and Drumm. "Anybody who calls me and tells me he's solved a murder and then starts tellin' me about a play called Volperoney or something has got to be either nuts or drunk. And you got a rep for the sauce, McGuffin."

"Not when I'm on a case," McGuffin said, going to the phone. He dialed the emergency number and got an answer after two rings. "This is Amos McGuffin speaking," he said. "Officer Chan and I are holding four murderers in a house in the Malibu Colony. Could you send—" McGuffin looked at Chan and shook his head. "He wants to know if you're *Charlie* Chan."

"Happens all the time," Chan muttered, as he walked to the phone. He handed McGuffin the gun and took the phone. "This is Detective Pedro Chan speaking," he began, slowly and politely. "And please, please do not tell me you're number one....I told you not to tell me that!" he shouted.

McGuffin settled himself in the Eames chair with the gun pointing casually in the direction of the prisoners. It was beginning to look like a long wait.